SET IN MOTION

SET IN

Valerie

NEW YORK

MOTION

Martin

Farrar, Straus and Giroux

For Robert

He may not come when you want him,
but he's right on time.

—Gospel hymn

SET IN MOTION

.

❋ 1

That morning Clarissa called and invited me to visit. I hadn't heard from her in some time and I was glad to accept the invitation. She had been my thesis adviser a few years earlier, when I was toying with the idea of continuing in academia. During the long interviews we shared, trying vainly to find something in literature that would yield itself to my limited powers of investigation, we had become good friends. We agreed that I would take the bus up on Friday afternoon, but on Thursday, when I saw Reed, he offered me his car. I set out on Friday evening, looking forward to the respite of a few days in the country. Clarissa lived north of the town itself, in an old farmhouse, surrounded by uncultivated fields and the irreversible decay of rural Louisiana.

The highway between New Orleans and Baton Rouge is a new one, cut through the Bonnet Carre spillway, a wide, modern, uncluttered strip of elevated road surrounded by swamp. There are no billboards, because it would be impractical to put them up in the swamp, where they would sink. That night there was almost no traffic and I allowed myself to sink into a reverie, induced by the swamp, the stifling humidity, and the heat. The entire drive takes about two hours. I had driven for perhaps twenty minutes when I became aware of some difficulty in holding the car to a straight course. I pulled over and got out, thinking that perhaps a tire had gone flat. There were no lights on the highway, save the mysterious circle of my own headlights. As I crossed in front of the car I heard a rushing of air just behind me and turned in time to see a large crane snapping in his long white wings as he settled just beyond the road at the water's edge. It was so dark I could barely make out the trees, but his white body stood out, iridescent against the black. I forgot about the tire and leaned against the rail. Looking down, I discovered two more cranes only a few yards away from me. There was no sound. Gradually I became aware of a strong wind moving among the trees. My hair was blowing back from my face. Why had I failed to notice it? It was the wind, I thought, that had caused the trouble with the car. I felt foolish for having stopped, but at the same time pleased that I had taken the time to look out across the spillway. I breathed deeply the damp black air and reflected that it wasn't unpleasant to be alone in the night with a destination secure ahead of me.

As I turned away from the rail, I nearly collided with a black woman who was standing in the glare of the headlights. My heart sent a little shout through my body, my knees went completely weak, so weak that I leaned against the car for support. The woman didn't move but stood looking at me. "God," I said, "you frightened me."

"I'm sorry," she said, stepping out of the light so that

I could no longer make out her face. "I didn't mean to scare you."

I looked up and down the road. There were no other cars in sight. "Where did you come from?" I asked.

She pointed up the road. "Laplace."

"But how?"

"I been walking," she replied impatiently.

"In this dark?"

"It weren't dark when I started." She backed away from me and leaned against the rail. "Where you goin' to?"

"Baton Rouge."

"I'm going back," she continued. "You take me back in your car?"

"I don't understand."

"I changed my mind. I'm goin' back. But I cain't walk 'cause I'm too tired."

I couldn't make out her face, but her voice was slow with fatigue. I was overcome by a variety of suspicions. What was she doing out here? Was someone with her, perhaps on the other side of the car, waiting to catch me off guard? Again I looked up and down the road. There were no other cars in sight. "Damn," I said aloud.

The woman turned her back to me and I looked out over the water. One of the cranes rose up, extinguished to a point of white as it whirled past the trees. The woman pressed her knuckles into her eyes, then pulled at her hair in desperation. "You gotta help me now," she said without turning toward me. "I cain't go no further."

I walked away from her, around the car. There was no one on the other side, but this revelation only served to increase my annoyance. Who was this woman? What did she want with me? She turned to face me, clinging

5

to the rail for support. The wind lifted her pale skirt around her knees and she attempted to hold it down with her free hand. I could think of no reason why I should not get in the car and drive off, leaving her as I had found her. I had the sensation that something was about to go dreadfully wrong. Occasionally, when looking at someone who is, perhaps, looking past my own shoulder, the expression on the other's face has filled me with this fear, that in the next moment something horrible will happen. I remembered hearing of a film about a night when the dead came back to life and set out to destroy everyone within a mile of the cemetery. I was told that what made this film frightening was that it showed people going about their everyday business unaware of danger until it was too late. That is how, I suspect, a great fear comes, always without warning. And that was what I expected to happen when I turned to the woman and said, "Get in," opening the door on my side and taking my place at the wheel. She didn't hesitate, but pulled the door open and slipped in beside me.

We drove for perhaps five minutes without speaking. She sat with her hands in her lap, absently wringing an old handkerchief, looking straight ahead at the road. From time to time I glanced at her, but she seemed uninterested in me. It was impossible to tell much about her in the dark. She could have been very young, I couldn't tell. Her stomach bulged out peculiarly beneath the threadbare material of her dress. Perhaps she was pregnant. Finally I could stand the silence between us no longer.

"You want to go back to Laplace?" I asked.

She gave no sign of having heard me. She resented

me, I thought, resented having to be dependent on me to get back to wherever she had come from.

"You comin' from the city?" she said at last.

"From New Orleans, yes."

"I was goin' there."

"Have you ever been there?"

"This here is the furthest I ever been."

"Do you have family there?"

She regarded me curiously in the darkness. I saw that she was smiling, a slow weary smile, such as a mother might give a child who continually asks why?

"You want to know about me?"

I didn't, really, want to know anything about her. I imagined that I could guess what had happened. She had tired of her country life, of the poverty of it, of the futurelessness of it, and longed now to live in the city. If she had family in the city, she was going to them. If she didn't, she was probably going to the Welfare Department.

"Sure," I said. "I want to know about you."

"Why?"

"Why not?" I countered.

"You going up to that college?"

"No. I'm going to visit a friend."

"I don't know nobody in that city. Tha's why I turned back."

"You almost made it, you know."

"How much further?"

"You would've been in the parish in another hour. And then twelve miles to get downtown."

"I almost made it," she agreed. "You want to take me to the city?"

"No. I'm not going there now. Not for a few days."

"You want me to get out of your car," she observed matter-of-factly.

"I don't care."

"I got nothing to go to that city for and I got nothing to go back for." She said this as if the idea had some appeal for her. "And tha's a fact."

"You have no family?"

"Maybe I ought to go on up to that Baton Rouge."

"You can, if you want. I'll take you up there."

"I'll go on up there, then."

I thought about what she would find there, trying to decide where the best place to leave her would be. Baton Rouge was no place for a black woman alone, but it probably wouldn't be a lot worse than where she was coming from. If I dropped her off in the black section of town, she might have a good chance of finding someone who could help her. There wasn't much work in the town, particularly for Negroes. She might get housework, if she was lucky. The white people there would treat her indifferently, even maliciously, but I imagined she was used to that sort of thing.

"What will you do up there?" I asked, without much hope of an enlightening reply. It was impossible to get a straight answer out of her.

"I'll find my way," she responded. I determined to let the silence that now fell between us turn to liquid before I would venture into it again. "I found my way this far," she added, reassuring herself.

We drove on in silence. The woman continued to wring her ragged handkerchief. She was becoming more agitated. Her hands pressed harder and harder against one another through the ragged cloth. The wind outside made it necessary for me to pay careful attention to my driving. When I glanced at her, I saw a tear trembling on the edge of her cheekbone, glistening in the dark. "For Christ's sake," I said. She gave a little shudder and turned her face away from me. "Please don't cry," I demanded. Now we were going to have an emotional explosion. I would have to stop the car. I would wind up looking after this poor creature for the rest of my life. It was more than I could stand. "Don't cry," I said again.

"I ain't cryin'," she sniffed.

"Good," I replied.

Ten minutes later we were driving through Laplace. I pulled into a gas station and told the attendant to fill the tank. I asked my passenger if she wanted a Coke, fully expecting the helpless shaking she gave her head, her eyes fastened upon her handkerchief. I thought it best to leave her alone for a few minutes so that she could regain her composure. As I got out of the car I asked her name.

"Ella," she said.

The wind had increased since the last time I had been out of the car. I went into the station and nodded to a young black man who was sitting behind a desk. "Is there a Coke machine in here?"

He regarded me suspiciously. "A what?"

"A Coke machine."

He pointed to the garage. I found the machine and stood drinking my Coke, relieved to be out of the wind. When I went back to the car, Ella was not in it. The man at the desk followed me and we stood exchanging money on the little island. I assumed that Ella had gone into the restroom. When the man turned away to wash the windshield, I got back in the car. I waited for perhaps five minutes, then went back into the station to see if the key to the restroom was gone. I found it hanging on the wall over the desk. The man had finished with the window by this time and ambled back into his office.

"Did you see the woman who was in the car with me?" I asked. He walked past me and took his place at his desk.

"What woman?"

How could I describe her? It unnerved me to have to tell a black person that I could think of no better description than that consummate adjective. "A black woman," I blurted, covering for myself with the rest of the description, "about my size, in a light-blue dress."

The man smiled to himself devilishly. "Where you comin' from?" he asked.

"Have you seen her?"

He shook his head. I went to the side of the station and tried the door to the restroom. It was open, but there was no one inside. I walked out to the highway and looked up and down it. There was no one walking in either direction. Perhaps she had gotten into another car, I thought. Or perhaps she had decided to stay in Laplace and had taken some road I didn't know about. I went back to the car and stood by the door. The man in the station watched me uninterestedly. The other man leaned against the pump and wiped his glasses with a paper towel.

"Did you see the woman I came in with?" I asked him.

He adjusted his glasses and threw the paper in the oil can. "What woman?" he said, smiling.

He was in on it, I decided. It was some kind of game they had come up with, the three of them. I got in the car without looking at either of the men again, and drove off down the highway.

Forty minutes later I was in Baton Rouge. Clarissa lived a mile north of the town and I drove this distance without stopping. There was almost no traffic, the population being of the most unimaginative inclinations, particularly about the night. When I pulled into Clarissa's drive I was startled to see the house dark. I left the car and walked to the back door. I felt oppressed, both by the experience with the woman on the highway and by my growing certainty that the house was empty. I knocked on the door and stood waiting for an answer. Nothing disturbed the humid darkness around me. I put my ear to the door. There was no sound inside. As my eyes grew accustomed to the dark, I made out a sinewy motion in the grass just beyond the step. Soundlessly, the shining black back of a large snake drifted into my focus. I turned again to the door, twisting the knob and beating on the wood. Perhaps something was wrong inside. Perhaps something had happened to Clarissa. Again I stood still in the darkness, watching the snake slither away under the house. I found a broom on the porch, and rustling the grass before me with the long stick, I made my way back to the car. I couldn't think what to do next. Why would she have called me if she wasn't going to be there? Surely something unexpected had happened to her.

I sat in the car for a few moments. It was possible that she had been delayed at the university, that she hadn't had time to get in touch with me. It was 9 p.m. Ordinarily such a situation would be unlikely, but I remembered that Clarissa had told me of a young professor who stayed in his office until ten every night, working

11

on a book about Dreiser. "In an empty building," she had added. Her pleasure in this idea suggested to me the possibility that she was attracted to the man. Perhaps he would be there. Perhaps he would know where she was.

I drove to the university. There were a few people about, coming out of evening classes. I went into the building where Clarissa's office was. The first-floor corridor was lit. An old black man pushing a rolling pail of water passed me. I ran up the stairs and stopped on the landing. The hall was dark before me. At the far end, a door stood open, flooding a small square of inviting light across the floor and walls. I walked quickly toward it, the sound of my shoes against the marble floor announcing my approach. When I stood full in the light, I looked into the open door, right into the most surprising eyes I have ever encountered.

The light seemed to be coming from him. His hair was light, long, surrounding his face in a full beard, so that he looked out from a circle of gold. His eyes were startlingly blue, light, wide, looking as if they could not believe what they saw. Reed would have called them "cocaine eyes," and this thought made me smile.

"Can I help you?" he inquired.

"I'm looking for Clarissa Pendleton."

"Really?"

"What do you mean, really?"

He stood up. "You'd better come in here and sit down."

I stepped back.

"You look very upset," he continued.

I laughed. "Christ," I said. "I've been having the most horrible time."

He indicated a chair, motioning me into it with a gesture of his hand. I sat down. "Do you know where she is?"

He smiled. "Clarissa?"

"Yes, Clarissa."

"No." He smiled again. "I don't know where she is."

I tried to gauge the degree of my frustration. It was remarkably intense.

"Where are you coming from?" he asked.

"New Orleans."

"And you came to see Clarissa."

"She called me," I explained. "She told me to come up tonight. I went to her house, there's no one there."

He considered this. "What will you do now?" he asked after a pause.

I looked at my hands. "I don't know."

"It seems a shame to come all the way up here, then turn around and go back."

"I guess I may as well," I replied, standing up.

"Sit down," he said authoritatively. I obeyed. "I'll be through here in a few minutes. Then I'll take you to get some coffee, if you like. By that time she may be home. You can call her."

"All right."

He nodded, then returned his attention to the page in front of him. He picked up his pen and wrote a few words. "What's your name?" he asked, without looking up.

"Helene."

"Helene," he repeated, testing the sound of it. "A friend of Clarissa's?"

"Does that seem strange?"

He looked up at me, meeting my gaze so directly that

I looked away. "Just a few minutes," he said. "And I'll be through here. Then we'll talk."

I looked around the room. The wall behind his desk was almost entirely covered with a rubbing of some monument. It showed a tall figure, draped in a black hooded cloak opened at the front to reveal a grinning skull. The hands were long bones, closed around one another. Another skull regarded me from the desk, the mouth slightly ajar, two of the lower teeth carefully removed to create a rest for the cigarette which smoldered inside the mouth. One wall was lined with books. On another wall a small bulletin board displayed two photographs of a motorcycle, front and side, and a few letters pinned to the cork with white tacks. I returned my gaze to the rubbing, staring into its black sockets, until he became aware of me again. "A friend of mine," he said, inclining his head toward the picture.

I turned my attention to him. "Should I know your name?"

"Michael." He looked as if this question annoyed him.

"Perhaps I should go," I concluded.

"No. I'm finished now. We can talk."

We walked across the campus to the student center. After the dark, quiet walkways, the lights in the cafeteria were unnerving. Michael went into the line to get coffee while I stopped to call Clarissa. When I joined him at the table, he was stirring sugar into a cup of unnaturally black coffee.

"Was there any answer?" he asked.

"No."

"You can call again in a while."

I opened my cream packet and poured it into my coffee. "I don't know. Maybe I should go back now."

14

"Now?"

"I don't know anyone else here. Even if I leave now it'll be late when I get back. I hate to drive when I'm sleepy."

"And you'll be depressed when you get back. Making this long trip for nothing."

"I guess so."

"Don't go back," he said, after a pause.

"I'll have to."

"Stay with me. You can stay with me tonight."

"But I don't know you."

He gulped the last of his coffee. "Take a chance," he said, pulling his coat over his shoulders. "Maybe Clarissa will come back. You can keep trying, anyway. And if she doesn't, it doesn't matter."

"What's your last name."

"Will it make a difference?"

I shrugged.

"Let's go then. We can get something to eat on the way."

"On the way where?"

"To my house."

His house was a pristine affair, with white walls, glass and metal furniture, orderly cases of books. "Call Clarissa," he said, pointing to the phone before he disappeared into the kitchen. I listened to the phone ring six times, then hung up. Michael came in carrying two glasses. "What is it?" I asked.

"Ginger ale," he said. "Is that O.K.?"

I followed him to the living room and sat across a table from him. He opened a canister and took out a small pipe. "Smoke?" he inquired.

I nodded. I didn't try to call Clarissa again. He played

15

records, string quartets and madrigals. Something about him bothered me. He invited me to relax, but refused to allow it. I felt disappointed. We sat in relative quiet for perhaps an hour. Occasionally he interjected a question, usually one I could answer with a simple yes or no. Then he stood up and gestured toward the back of the house. "Shall we go to bed?" he suggested. I followed him to the bedroom. When he flicked on the light I found myself relieved. Here was a room one could relax in. The others must have been for show. The large brass bed was unmade, two books lay open on the sheets. There were rugs on the floor, strewn with ashtrays, a glass, and a coffee cup. The books were simply piled into the corners. He crossed ahead of me and sat on the bed, surveying the room. "It's a mess in here," he said. I stood in the doorway, looking around me, trying to get some kind of bearing. What was I expecting?

I wasn't expecting what I found when I met his gaze. His look was so cold, so impassive, that I stepped back. "What are you doing?" he asked.

I laughed weakly. "I don't know."

He crossed the room quickly and stood just in front of me. "Does it seem a little abrupt to you?"

"I'm afraid so."

"And yet, when you came to my office, you acted as if you were looking for me."

"I was, in a way. To find out about Clarissa. She told me you would be there. That you always work late."

"And what else?"

"And nothing else."

"Oh." He smiled. "Then she didn't tell you about me?"

"Does she know something I should know?"

"At this point? No. I don't think so."

"You make me feel very foolish."

He touched my shoulder tentatively. To avoid becoming as confused as I suspected I might, I put my hands on his shoulders and kissed him. I felt something in that embrace that surprised me. It was as if I had struck him. He weakened, in the way women are supposed to weaken at the touch of their beloved. At the same time I was sure that he wasn't experiencing any intense pleasure, or even surprise. It was the touch, what he had waited for. I sensed that it always affected him in this way, weakened him, and that he resented it. When he released me I leaned against the wall and looked at a spot just past his shoulder. He pressed his palm against the small of my back and propelled me through the doorway. I felt a wave of confidence rushing through me. I would be able to handle it. Nothing unexpected would happen. I turned around to look at him, smiling, confident, expecting to be folded into another exploratory embrace. He stood still in the doorway, with the same cold regard that had unnerved me before. "Take off your clothes," he said, then came toward me, casually unbuttoning his shirt. I undressed quickly and slipped beneath the blankets while he was still untying his shoes. He sat on the edge of the bed and I wrapped myself around him, rubbing my cheek against his back. He pulled off his socks, then, raising himself slightly from the bed, pulled off his pants in one long motion. I put my hand in his lap, fingers closing tremulously around a rigid erection. So there would be no trouble with that, I told myself. I would rather almost anything than trouble with that. He turned toward me abruptly and pulled the sheet away. I smiled, stretching beneath his hands, and closed my eyes, dizzy with anticipation.

17

"I'm cold," I said after a few moments. I opened my eyes. He was watching his hand as he moved it over my breasts, down to my waist, then quickly around to the back of my thigh. "Very nice," he said, appraising me. With both hands wedged behind my thighs, he began to press the muscles along the backs of my legs. I looked away, perhaps for a second, at the title of the book lying on the table next to the bed, *Ada,* Nabokov, and in the corner of that glance I saw him smile, a cruel, brutal little smile. Involuntarily my hands grasped for the brass posts above my head. In one deft and devastating motion he pulled my legs apart and rammed himself into me, deeply, suddenly, so that my arms stiffened to keep my head from being pushed through the brass bars. "Jesus," I whimpered.

I was so shocked by this rude force that, finding my mouth against his shoulder, I sank my teeth into the flesh as hard as I could. But he didn't pull back. Instead, catching my hair with one hand so that I couldn't turn away, he forced his shoulder farther into my mouth, with such insistence that, in fear for my teeth, I was forced to relax my grip. Then he drew back and looked down at me with an expression of aloof curiosity. I ran my tongue over my teeth and glanced at his shoulder, where the impression I had made was turning scarlet. He looked at this mark too, without surprise, then back at me. We smiled at each other. All this happened in a moment, but our smiles communicated that it had been a moment appreciated by both.

I wrapped my legs tightly around his back and put my arm across his shoulder. He hid his face in the pillow beside my head. In this position, for a full fifteen minutes, I encouraged his assault. I concentrated on relaxing, and on following the rapid plunging of his hips with my own. Gradually the pain lessened, dispersed, turned into a liquid pleasure. By the time he was done, my physical responses had resolved themselves into an unconscious accuracy. When he rose to his knees, pulling me with him for a final convulsive drive, I laughed out loud, such was my excitement. I saw his face then, his lips drawn back over his teeth, his eyes wide and startled, before he fell down again across me, breathing heavily.

I kept still beneath him, waiting. What was he thinking? He was marveling, I thought, left speechless. I imagined that he would say something, give me some compliment. I ran my tongue along his shoulder, enjoying the salt, then moved my legs a little. He followed my motion. Perhaps he would want to start all over again. My limbs were trembling with exhaustion, but, yes, I thought, I would be willing.

Another minute passed. I sensed that he had some reason for keeping his face averted from mine. What was his expression? I imagined a frightening grimace, and this picture made me laugh.

He rolled off me, turning his back to me. "What's so funny?" he asked, and the contempt in his voice filled me with anxiety. What had it been for him? A performance? An obligation? An act of mercy? I turned away without answering, curling my knees up to my stomach. I hoped I wouldn't start rocking. When I started rocking I knew I was really scared. And I didn't want him to know how badly he had hurt me. I lay still; I had to make an effort to do so, and the effort kept me awake. I waited until I was certain that he was asleep. Then I got out of bed, gathered my clothes, and crept into the hall. I put my pants on and pulled my dress over my head, transferring my sandals from one hand to the other as I pushed my arms through the sleeves. In the living room I buttoned the front of my dress and sat down by the phone. I dialed Clarissa's number.

Her phone had rung three times when I saw him in the doorway.

"What are you doing?" he asked.

I stood up. "Calling Clarissa."

"Clarissa's in Mobile, visiting her parents."

I hung up the phone and looked at him blankly. He was naked, one hand resting against the frame of the doorway. "Didn't you know?" he asked.

I sat down and pulled on my sandals. My purse was lying on the floor next to the chair. I opened it, pulled out a brush, and ran it through my hair. Michael didn't move.

"Go back to bed," I said. "You're asleep on your feet."

He turned away. "Come back with me," he said. "It doesn't matter."

I waited until he had reached the end of the hall. Then I grabbed my purse, crossed the room, and opened the front door, pulling it closed quietly behind me.

I ran. Reed's car was parked in the street and I ran to it. When I pulled the door open I glanced in the back seat to make sure no one was lying there, waiting for me. I locked myself in and started the car. I saw the light go on in Michael's room as I pulled away from the curb. The streets were dark, the town was quiet. I concentrated on driving through it as quickly as possible. When I turned into the last approach to the highway, I saw a man walking toward a parked car on the side of the road, holding an electric lantern out in front of him.

As I passed him he turned and waved at me with his free hand. I didn't remember that I had seen his face then, clearly, suddenly, until I crossed the Orleans parish line, two hours later.

❋ *2*

I went straight home. I had never run so long, so intently, from an inarticulated fear before. It was nearly three when I turned out the lights in my apartment. When I closed my eyes I had already half settled into the dream I would conjure for the rest of the night.

Clarissa called from Mobile the next morning. Her mother was very ill, she explained; the doctor had called her Friday evening and told her to come at once. "I tried to call you but I guess you'd already left," she said. "Did you find my note?"

I said that I hadn't seen it, perhaps it had been blown away.

"I stuck it to the back door," she said.

"I guess I didn't see it," I said.

"You must be put out with me."

"No. I don't know why I didn't see it. It's my own fault."

"What did you do?"

"I turned around and went home," I said.

"Helene, I'm really sorry."

"It doesn't matter. I enjoyed the drive. How's your mother?"

"She's much better, By the time I got there she felt good enough to scold me for coming. I'm going back this afternoon."

"I'm glad," I said.

We talked a little more. I agreed to visit her sometime in the next month.

"Is everything all right?" she asked when we had settled this.

"Of course," I protested. "Of course I'm all right."

After this conversation I drove downtown to return Reed's car to him. I had difficulty finding a space and had to park on Esplanade. As I got out of the car, I saw Maggie's husband, Richard, walking toward me. I suspected that he would pretend he didn't know me, though we had seen each other often enough, at work, when he came to pick up Maggie. They had even driven me to my apartment on two occasions. I didn't like him and suspected that he returned this sentiment. As he drew near he began to smile. I nodded, expecting him to go by with no more greeting than this. I was surprised when he stopped and, with another slow, rather shy smile, inquired, "How are you?"

"All right," I said. "And you?"

"Hot." He shaded his eyes with his hands and winced at the sun. "I'll walk down with you," he said, pointing toward the Quarter. "If you don't mind."

I asked him where he was going and he shrugged. "Nowhere," he said. "Maggie's at her mother's. I got bored at home."

I felt uncomfortable walking with him. He made himself pleasant to me and I sensed that he was up to something. At the same time I couldn't help responding to his apparent need for company. When we arrived at St. Philip Street I asked him where he would go next.

Again he put his hands over his eyes and squinted at the sun. I imitated this gesture, and we stood together in the street, looking up into the intense blue of the sky. He leaned against a car. "I'd like to take you to lunch," he said. "But I don't have any money."

His manner was jocular enough, but there was a note of pleading in his voice that disturbed me. I felt, without a doubt, that I should go straight to Reed's apartment, which was only a few blocks away. Instead I found myself telling Richard that I would be pleased to take him to lunch.

As we walked on I began to regret my invitation. He was quiet, considering what to do with my company now that he had it. "I suppose you and I should get to know one another," he said. "Since Maggie is so fond of you."

"Are you trying to convince yourself?" I responded without thinking.

"I feel I *should* talk to you."

"What can we talk about," I said, "since we've made such a bad start?"

"You can tell me what Maggie tells you," he said.

"That wouldn't be very fair to her."

"Then she tells you things she wouldn't tell me."

I began to resent him. "If you want to have lunch with me so you can pump me about your wife, maybe we should forget the whole thing."

"We don't have to talk about Maggie. We can talk

25

about anything. We can talk about anything at all."
Again I felt his levity disguised some deeper concern,
not for me, but for our conversation.

I was unable to think of anything to say. We walked
along in silence until we reached the restaurant. It was
the LaForge patio, where Maggie and I often lunched
together.

As we sat down I was aware of the unsettled question
between us. I had made it clear that I didn't wish to talk
to him about Maggie, but in doing this it was possible
that he thought I wanted to talk about myself, or more
particularly, about "us." This was not my intention. I
didn't want him to ask me about myself, nor did I want
to make any observations about our being together.

I could see that he was as worried as I was. He twirled
his napkin around and commented on the great crawling vine that threatened to engulf our table. I would
have been content to have our lunch without speaking,
but I couldn't tell him this.

"It's strange," he said. "You and I having lunch together."

There it was, the subject of "us." I was spared a reply
to this remark by the appearance of the waiter. We or-
dered drinks and our lunch and sat looking at one another.

"You don't know how difficult it is for me to sit here
with you," he said when the drinks came. Then, as if
this remark was an explanation for what he was about
to do, he drained off half of his drink.

"I don't know why you should feel threatened by me,"
I said.

"It's because you know something about me. And I
don't know what that something is."

I could understand his uncertainty. I felt that I did indeed know something about him, but as I watched him clutching his glass, I recognized the probability that I knew nothing at all. "I haven't passed any judgment on you," I told him, "if that's what you're worried about. And Maggie hasn't told me anything particularly revealing about you." This was a lie and it surprised me.

"Maggie isn't very happy with me," he said flatly.

"She's never told me that."

"No. I doubt that she would complain of me. No more than she would complain of a persistent insect."

"You think she ignores you?"

"She's bored with me."

"You've been married a long time," I said. "I think boredom is bound to set in."

He affected surprise. "You argue against marriage?"

"For myself," I said. "Only for myself."

"Because you would lose interest."

"Because I doubt that I could inspire continued interest."

"What a shabby defense," he said. "I think you must not be in the habit of doing it."

"Defending myself?" I thought it over. "No," I said, "I suppose I don't very often."

"Because you've nothing to defend."

I imagined myself as a fish, working a hook deeper and deeper into my bleeding jaws. My answer was well considered. "Everyone has something they have to save for themselves," I said. "And when that's threatened, and I think it invariably happens in marriages that it *is* threatened, then everything becomes intolerable."

As I delivered myself of this wisdom, the lunch arrived. Richard sat quietly while the waiter set the plates before us. He asked if we would like more drinks, and though I had already decided that one would be more than enough, I nodded. Richard, giving me a sidelong look, nodded as well. After the waiter had gone he picked up his fork and stabbed at his omelette.

"That's true," he said.

It took me a moment to realize that he was responding to my last remark. Now, I saw, we would have to finish our lunch with this self-indulgent understanding between us. No one could be content for long with anyone else. Would there be nothing for us but to fall into one another's arms on this note?

"But Maggie doesn't know that," Richard said.

"No," I agreed. "No, she doesn't."

"I do the best I can," he continued. "I don't want her to be unhappy with me. I try . . ."

"She knows that," I said. "I'm sure she appreciates that."

He looked at me suspiciously. "I don't like the idea that she confides her little troubles to you. I would like to put a stop to that."

This abrupt change in mood startled me. I began to get an idea of what Maggie was up against. "If she doesn't tell me," I said, "she'll tell someone else. Why shouldn't she? It doesn't do any harm."

"How do you know what harm it does?" he said sharply. "She's worse now than she ever was. She's all discontent. I can't please her. I can't please myself."

I felt a twinge of panic at this. I didn't want to be anybody's confidante. What I wanted was to confide my own troubles to someone. What was it about me that unleashed these wretched confessions from otherwise sensible people?

"If you start to confide in me, too," I said, "it will be too uncomfortable."

Our eyes met, held for a moment, and I was aware of a curious sympathy stretching between us. He reached across the table and touched my cheek. "I'm sorry," he said. "I've been thinking of you as the enemy."

"It doesn't matter," I said.

He seemed annoyed by this easy absolution. "I don't like to be alone in the afternoons," he said. "Particularly on the street. And at home, too. I get very restless. I have to go out. But seeing strangers on the street only makes it worse. When I saw you, I thought I might get you to stay with me for the afternoon, and then I wouldn't have to think about these . . . unnatural feelings."

I knew that I shouldn't encourage this kind of talk, but my curiosity was aroused. "What is it that frightens you?" I asked.

"It's not really fear. I have difficulty getting underway, getting into motion."

"Whenever I stand at the top of a staircase, I always pause before going down," I said. "It's as if I were frozen."

He gave me a sympathetic look. "Yes, yes, that's it."

"Thinking about it makes it worse."

"Yes," he said again, as if he were talking to himself. "Trying not to think about it makes it worse still."

I felt uneasy myself, by our sudden rapprochement. Where would we go from there? We finished our lunch, and when I spotted the waiter lurking behind a palm, I suggested that we should go. Richard folded his napkin and put his hands in his lap like a child. I paid the waiter and we went out into the street together.

When the sunlight hit me I was confused. I stumbled

over the curb and Richard took my elbow, guiding me onto the sidewalk. We walked along for perhaps a block before he spoke.

"Would you come home with me?" he asked.

I pulled away from him and slammed right into the wall of the Ursuline convent. Was I drunk? I thought. Had I heard him correctly? He didn't try to reclaim me, and so I stood for a few moments, my head against the wall, trying to regain my sense of proportion. I was struck by the ferocity of my feelings. I found myself thinking, Be sensible, be reasonable, as if I could conjure some drifting spirit of common sense. I turned to face him, still leaning against the wall for support. He stood rubbing his hands together. If he had smiled I would have known what to do. But he didn't smile. He looked into my eyes with such intensity that I felt he was reading my thoughts. I smiled weakly. Still he didn't smile. I began to wonder how long we could stand this before one of us made a move. I had a strong desire to run. Gradually the expression on his face changed. He was invaded as he stood there; his hands trembled, his eyes glazed over with some internal vision. I felt that he was no longer aware of my presence.

Perhaps, I thought, he was only asking me to stay with him to help keep away the nervous agitation he was now experiencing. It would be a sin to leave another soul in this condition. I put my hand over his, trying to calm myself while imposing a distance between us. "No," I said, hardly aware of what I was doing. "No, no, no."

He took a cue from this and drew away, though he didn't take his hand from mine. Now, I thought, we would extricate ourselves from each other.

"I'm going back down," he said, pointing to the Quarter. "I'm going back down there. I'll leave you here."

"Will you be all right?" I asked. I felt as if I were sending him off into a nightmare.

"Yes, I'll be all right. There's always someone I know on the street. I'll go back down, find somebody I know."

"I'm sorry," I said. "I wish I could, but I can't. I just can't."

He was in control of himself again. I released his hand and he shaded his eyes from the sun. Then he looked at me and smiled. "What are we talking about?" he said.

I laughed. The spell was broken. I straightened and shuddered as I felt a trickle of sweat moving down my back.

"Thank you for the lunch," he said.

"My pleasure." I sounded weaker than he. Which one of us was responsible for this? I thought.

He took a few steps, nodding at me complicitously, then turned and walked rapidly away. I stood for a moment, allowing the hot August sun its devastation; then walked to Reed's apartment.

Reed answered the door only half awake, a towel wrapped around his waist. "You're back early," he said.

I followed him to the kitchen and looked over his shoulder as he examined the contents of the refrigerator.

"Do you want me to cook you something?" I asked.

"No. I'm just going to drink some milk. I'll put some of this instant shit in it."

I laughed.

"What's funny?"

"Instant shit."

"Why are you back early?" he asked, stirring the brown powder into his milk.

I sat down at the table. "I came back last night."

"How come? You had a fight with your friend?"

"She wasn't there."

"You're very nervous, you know."

I frowned and pulled the newspaper across the table, pretending to read. He got up and went to the sink, drinking the last of his milk. Then he took some yellow capsules from a drawer, opened two of them, and poured the powder into a spoon. I put down the paper and watched him. "What is it?" I asked.

He came back to the table, bringing the spoon, a small syringe, and a glass of water. "Nembutal," he said. "I got it last night. Sixty dollars. I could sell it for two hundred."

"You going to sell it?"

He drew the clear liquid into the syringe. "I'll let you know in a minute."

I went to the refrigerator and poured myself a glass of orange juice. When I sat down again, Reed had tied my scarf around his arm and was injecting the liquid. I watched it go in; then the blood came out. His face was intent. "This rig is so small," he said. "It won't be enough."

Nothing fascinated me more than watching Reed take drugs. I had witnessed the little scene he now played before me for three years and I had still not tired of it. I remembered the first time I had seen it, about a week after we had begun our endless affair. He had not asked me once, during that week, how I felt about drugs, what I took, nothing. One morning he got out of bed and pulled a small metal box out of the dresser drawer.

"What are you doing?" I inquired.

"I want to take this Methedrine," he said, brandishing a syringe. "Do you want some?"

I demurred, but sat next to him on the edge of the bed while he filled the syringe.

"Do you take that often?" I asked.

"I take what I can get."

"I don't think I've ever seen anyone do that before."

"It's nothing," he said, jabbing the needle into his arm. "It's like taking a pill."

I watched in silence. He drew the needle out. "You don't need to tell anybody about this."

I shrugged. "Who would I tell?"

Later I thought about the way he had chosen to give me this vital information about himself. It was flamboyant, to be sure, calculated to shock. But at the same time it was a long shot, for he had no reason to believe that I wouldn't run screaming from the room at the very thought of such an enterprise. So I saw it as kind of a trust, a pledge of trust, that he had revealed his weakness to me without fear of repercussions. I knew also that it was a warning to me. I didn't need to know very much about hard drugs to understand that they come before any other consideration for those who live under their demanding influence.

As far as I had been able to determine, he was not addicted to anything in particular, but I could think of nothing he hadn't tried. I always expected something to go wrong. I was, in fact, waiting for him to stand up and drop dead. That was the pact between us, that I enjoyed watching his random attempts at suicide, not because I wanted him to die, but because it was, to me, such a magnificent and casual gesture at death, and I applauded that gesture. He had long since given up trying to get me to join him in his explorations. I watched, I asked how everything felt, I was an authority on the effects of different drugs, but I didn't have the courage to participate.

He dropped the syringe into the glass of water and fell back in his chair.

"How is it?" I asked.

He looked at me blankly, then smiled, as if he saw me dimly, through a pleasant haze. I sat watching him over my orange juice, for perhaps a minute. He began to talk, slowly, with long pauses, about a camera he had seen. "It's secondhand," he explained, ". . . but it's in good shape . . . it's got three really good lenses, fine lenses . . . a telescopic lens . . . I could shoot . . . clear across town."

"How much is it?"

"He wants four hundred. I think I could get it for three-fifty."

"Do you have that much?"

"If I sell this stuff . . . I hate to sell it . . . I could use the money to get this morphine that's coming in . . . and then I can sell that, really high . . . I can get enough."

He stood up abruptly and took the glass with the syringe back to the sink. "This rig is too small," he said.

"You O.K.?"

He turned, leaning against the counter in obvious need of its support. "What happened to you in Baton Rouge?" he asked. "Why'd you come back early?"

I shrugged. "It's all involved," I said.

"No, tell me. Tell me what happened."

I told him about Michael. When I finished my story he

took his seat across from me. "Why did you do that?" he asked.

"What part of it?"

"The whole thing. Why did you do it?"

I tried to think of some plausible explanation.

"Never mind," he said after a moment. "I know. I've done it myself, a hundred times."

I put my head in my hands.

"You depressed now, huh." He rubbed his hands clumsily against my skull.

"I don't know. I guess so."

He pulled the newspaper from the chair beside mine and thumbed through the pages. "I'm off tonight. You want to go to the movies? They have one of those foreign films, like you like, at the Peacock. That might cheer you up."

"What is it?" I asked without interest.

He spread the paper out before me and pointed to a small black square in the corner of the page. "How do you say it?"

I looked at the word, *Teorema.* "It's Italian," I said. "Te-o-rem-a, I guess. I've never heard of it."

"We'll go see it," he said, closing the paper. "It'll cheer you up."

That night I stayed with Reed. In the morning I had to take a bus uptown to change my clothes and take another bus back downtown to work. I was half an hour late. When I was writing the time on the sheet in the crowded hall, my supervisor came to her office door and signaled me to come in. "You're late," she said when I stood indifferently across the desk from her.

"I know. I got hung up."

35

"Try not to do it again."

I nodded. She picked up a stack of folders on her desk and nodded at them. "Can you come in for a conference between three and four this afternoon?"

"I've got a three-thirty appointment."

She ran her finger down a schedule on the desk, pursing her mouth. "I thought you were off this afternoon."

"It's just a woman who wants to bring in a note from her husband. Non-support. It was the only time we could agree on."

"All right. Come at three, we should be through in half an hour."

I nodded again. We stood looking at one another. I had very little feeling for this woman. Our relations were unstrained, businesslike. She smiled. "Do you know you processed more emergencies last month than anyone else in the department?"

"Really?" I said.

"Your luck, I guess." It was a joke between us. Two days a week I took emergency cases, and for reasons no one could explain, there were always twice as many crying, threatening people on these days. I had also, on occasion, offered to take cases when I was not on emergency duty, simply because no one else was available. My supervisor appreciated this. On my last evaluation she had written that I was a credit to the department, that I was exceptionally agreeable, making myself available for extra work whenever necessary. We both knew that this was because I had cultivated, after six months in the department, a studied indifference to the problems of my clients. I was efficient. I got satisfaction from processing as many people as I could, as quickly as possible. It made no difference to me whether they were coming on or off the rolls. My manner with the clients was straightforward, businesslike. It made it easier for them and they rarely complained of me.

My supervisor nodded, dismissing me. I decided to walk through the waiting room on my way to my desk, so that the receptionists would know I was in. When I stepped into the room a tall black woman stood up and touched my shoulder. "There she is," she said. "You my worker, aren't you?"

I looked up into her long, woebegone face. "I don't think so."

"You don't remember me?"

"What's your worker's name?"

"I don't know her name. What's your name?"

"Thatcher."

"That's it. You her."

"Do you have an appointment?" I asked, easing myself out of her grasp. I cast a long, helpless look at Kay, the receptionist, who was watching us.

"No, I don't need one. You made a mistake on this here." She opened her small cloth bag, an evening bag, probably given to her by someone she worked for. "Right here, on this, you made a mistake. I went down there to get my stamps and they said I couldn't get no stamps this month. 'Cause you made a mistake here on this date."

I looked at the card. "This is signed by Miss Durham," I said. "She's your worker."

She continued to hold the card out in front of me. "But it's a mistake. You made a mistake."

I glanced at the name on the top of the card. "Sit down, Mrs. Matthews," I said. "I'll go and tell Miss Durham you're here and she'll come talk to you about it."

37

"I been here since eight o'clock. I went down there yesterday to get my stamps and they made me wait for three hours."

The receptionist came up behind me. "Miss Thatcher," she said with unequivocal authority, "your eight-thirty is here." I nodded and began to back away from the woman. "Who is your worker?" she asked the woman, who stood holding her card out. "Let me see that card."

I turned away from them and went toward the switchboard. As I passed, the operator nodded at me. "You got a call waiting." I closed the smoky glass door behind me and went to my desk.

Maggie was standing to leave just as I sat down. "They're wild today," I said.

She smiled nervously and opened a case file in her hand. "I've turned this woman down three times already," she said, tapping her finger against the folder. "She keeps coming back." She grimaced. "Did you have a good weekend?"

"O.K. Strange."

"Strange?"

"I'll tell you later."

"I need to talk to you," she said.

"Is something wrong?"

"Yes. No. It's Richard. I'll tell you at lunch."

Maggie turned away just as my phone rang. I picked it up, opening my desk drawer and pulling out a sheaf of folders. "Miss Thatcher," I said.

"Miss Thatcher." An angry female voice assaulted me. "I been waiting on this phone for twenty minutes to talk to you."

"I'm sorry to keep you waiting. I just got in."

"I got this letter here and it say my food stamps been cut to $85 a month."

"Who is this, please?"

"This is Mrs. Davis," she said haughtily. I flipped through the cases on my desk. I had two Mrs. Davises.

"What's your first name, please?"

The voice paused for a moment, filling up with indignation. "This is Mrs. William Davis," she said, in a smothered rage. "And I got this letter in my hand here with your signature on the bottom of it and it say my stamps been cut to $85 a month."

I tried to remember Mrs. William Davis. It was hopeless. "One moment please, Mrs. Davis," I said. "Let me get your case." I shuffled through the folders in my hands again, then flipped quickly through a stack in the wire basket containing cases that had been approved by my supervisor. In the middle of this stack I found one with the name DAVIS, WILLIAM EMMA typed across the white tab. I pulled it out and opened it. It was a large case, probably a few years old. I flipped through the pages to the last entry. Mrs. Davis's daughter Belinda, I read, who was sixteen, had had a child three months earlier. At that time I had increased the amount of food stamps she received from $85 to $113 a month, to account for the new child. Two weeks ago, according to the last entry, Mrs. Davis had called to tell me that the child had died. At that time I had reduced the amount of stamps she would receive to $85 again. It was standard procedure. I wondered why it had taken two weeks for her to be notified of the change. I picked up the phone again.

"Mrs. Davis?" I said. I dreaded having to tell her the reason.

"I'm here," she said.

"I made that change two weeks ago, when you called to tell me that Belinda's baby had died."

"Do you mean to tell me that's why you done cut my stamps back to $85?" Outrage reduced her voice to a vicious whisper.

"I'm afraid so," I said. "I told you at that time that they would be cut back. The stamps are issued according to the number of people in the house. Now that Belinda's baby is no longer in the house, I have to issue the amount for a household of three people. There are only three people in the house now, aren't there?"

"There's me and Belinda, and Corina."

Why didn't she hang up on me? Didn't she realize that she would get no satisfaction from me? "$85 is the amount for a household of three."

"I shouldn't have told you that baby died. Belinda told me not to tell you. She said you'd do something like this. She said you'd try to cut us off."

"Mrs. Davis," I pleaded. "I'm sorry. It's not up to me. You were right to tell me. You signed an agreement when you first came here that said you would notify us immediately of any changes in the household as soon as they occurred. Now if you hadn't told me, I would have found out eventually and then you'd have had to pay back all the money that was issued to you for the baby, for as long as he wasn't there."

"I shouldn't have told you."

"You were right to tell me."

She sputtered. I steeled myself for the rush of hate that was about to come pouring out of the instrument I was holding to my ear. I heard an intake of breath, slow, painful, hopeless, and then a click as the receiver was placed carefully in its cradle. I glanced at the name on the top of the stack in front of me. My eight-thirty. Mr. Williams, who was waiting for me. I opened the case and looked at the top page. He was twenty-five years old and lived alone. That was unusual. I hung up the phone and walked to the waiting room. When I opened the door, a sea of black faces looked up at me expectantly, impatiently. I noticed the woman who had spoken to me earlier, still standing against the wall, her card clutched in her hand. "Mr. John Williams," I called.

In the back of the room I saw a man stand up and sit down again. Then the crowd parted and Mr. John Williams, a young man with dark, pockmarked skin; long, twisted arms that ended in convulsively twitching hands; and an expression of unrelieved pain, came rolling toward me, his wheelchair propelled by another young black man who eyed me, with unmistakable distrust, over the head of his disabled friend.

I met him at the edge of the crowd. "Right this way," I said to the man who was pushing the chair. In the hall I was forced to walk ahead of him, because of the crowd. When we reached the interview room I stepped back to let him go through. "In here," I said. Mr. Williams dropped his head back in his chair and rolled unfocused eyes at me as he went past. I felt a shudder, starting at the base of my spine, up my back. When it reached my neck, I shivered. The young man, who had drawn a chair up next to his friend's wheelchair, gave me a terse, unsympathetic smile. I closed the door and took my seat, opening the folder to look once again at the information sheet that had been prepared by the receptionist. "Is this the first time you've ever applied for food stamps?" I asked, directing my question to both men.

Mr. Williams hunched suddenly forward in his chair. His hands tore at one another in his lap and in his throat a curious whining began. He tried to look at me, but because of the tremendous effort required for him to shape a word, he failed. I sat in dismal suspense. Finally, his lips parted and a sound that could be identified as yes came forth. He fell back in his chair, exhausted by the effort.

I looked at his friend, and our eyes met. I saw in that glance that he wouldn't help me. His look was amused, contemptuous. I wanted to help people, it suggested; very well, then help this fellow who could not speak and who was hideously ugly.

I returned my attention to Mr. Williams. "It says here you live alone, in the Desire project?"

I hoped he would simply nod his head. Instead, he leaned forward in his chair again and repeated the horrible performance I had just witnessed. At the end of his struggle the monosyllable tore into the air. I felt a wave of tears pressing behind my eyes. I concentrated on the application before me.

It took twenty-five minutes to fill out the simple form I had to complete. In that time, by asking only questions that could be answered with a yes or a no, I learned that Mr. Williams lived alone in a rent-free apartment in the Desire project. I couldn't imagine his life there, in the worst project in the city, in two miserable rooms that were doubtless unheated, without hot water, probably without sufficient plumbing, and rat-infested. In these two rooms Mr. Williams sat in his chair and twitched, twenty-four hours a day. I didn't know how he got dressed. I assumed that his friend came in to help him. I didn't know how he had gotten there, or where he had been before, and I didn't try to find out. For the purpose of issuing food stamps all I needed to do was call the project office and ascertain that he did indeed live alone. They would also be able to verify Mr. Williams's statement that he had no income whatsoever. I imagined that his friend would take him out to get food stamps. If he went alone he would most certainly be robbed.

I explained the terms of the agreement to Mr. Williams and turned to his friend for a signature. The young man smiled and looked away. He was not signing anything. I didn't want to look at Mr. Williams, but an explosion of motion in his chair claimed my attention. He was drawing himself up, pulling his right arm out of his lap with the aid of his resisting left hand. At the same time the whining in his throat had begun again. He wished to speak. I looked at him with undisguised amazement. "Ag . . . sig," he said at last, by which I understood that he meant to sign the page himself. His friend was watching me now, his disgust at my reluctance filling the room like noxious gas. I stood up and moved around the table so that I was next to Mr. Williams. Oblivious to his friend, to my loathing, to everything except the line on the page that could not be processed without a signature, I took Mr. Williams's hand in my own and closed the pen beneath his fingers. I planned to make a quick X as soon as I got the pen to the line, but the trembling hand I held in my own made a struggle that culminated in something like a "J." So he wanted the whole name. Together we pulled the pen out of the "J" and into a tiny circle that might pass for an "o." His friend was watching us with interest now. Would we succeed? When we finished the word John, I pulled his hand up for a moment and allowed his fingers to relax their deathlike grip on the pen. Then we went down again. The "W" came out like an "N." When we had completed the second "l," I became aware of Mr. Williams's eyes, which had attached themselves to my face. Why was he looking at me? Why wasn't he looking at the line? I paused in the midst of the "i" and met his gaze.

I wasn't prepared for what I found in that look. There I saw his determination, and his pride, which would not be shaken, which would answer every question put to it, which would suffer anything, including the chilling indifference of a young white woman who was interested only in getting away from him, who was disgusted by the sight of him, horrified by the touch of him, which would suffer this and twenty times this to get his name down on a piece of paper by the effort of his uncontrollable fingers. I smiled at him. I didn't mean to smile. He had shamed me and he knew it, though he had not meant to. For a moment I thought I was going to put my arms around him and hold him close, for his courage, which I could not fathom, and for his patience, which was an animal's patience. There was nothing he could not suffer. He could suffer my embrace. His friend saw my confusion and sniffed. I looked up into his cold regard, and without speaking he told me what a white girl's mercy is worth. Mr. Williams's hand was still trembling—at the end of the "i." "We're almost through," I said. We made the "a" and then the long "m" and then the "s." "We did it," I said breathlessly. I released his hand, which he allowed to flutter on the page a moment, smudging the signature with interested fingertips. His friend leaned forward and looked at the signature. It was a child's scrawl, worse than that, but it could be made out as "John Williams." I drew the page away and slipped it into the folder. "That's all," I said. "You'll get your card in the mail in a few days."

His friend stood up and pulled the chair away from the table. I went to the door, opened it, and stood just inside as Mr. Williams rolled past me, out of the room. As he went by, I caught his friend's eye again. "Thank you," I said. What was I thanking him for? "For bringing him," I added.

He gave me an indifferent nod. "I take care of him," he said. I stood in the door, clutching my little folder to my chest as Mr. Williams and his friend disappeared down the hall.

❀ *3*

For the rest of the morning I labored with my shame. I hated myself and my work, because I was helpless and because I preferred to be helpless. By 11:30 I was in a miserable frame of mind. Maggie came in from her last interview and sat down. "Are you ready to go?" she asked.

I didn't want to talk, though if I had wanted to talk to anyone it would have been Maggie. "Where can we go?" I asked. "I need a drink."

We agreed to walk to LaForge's, where we could pass the time idly over cool drinks. As we made our way through the perpetually crowded halls and down the smudge-pink stairs of the Welfare Office, I held my breath against wave after wave of despair. Outside, we found the heat so oppressive that we decided to take a bus for the six short blocks to the Quarter.

"I think something's wrong with Richard," Maggie began, when we were seated in the patio.

"Is he sick?" I asked.

"No. It's not that. It's just that . . . he behaves very strangely."

"In what way?"

"Well, last night, at dinner. He had a pad of paper and he kept adding up a bunch of figures, over and over. When I asked him what he was doing, he said he was 'measuring the universe.' He was so involved in it, I didn't push it. Then after dinner he went out for a while, to see Sam, he said, about taking some measurements. I figured it was for a painting or something. When he came back he was anxious. I asked if he'd argued with Sam and he said he hadn't been at Sam's. Before I could find out where he'd been, he snatched up the book I was reading—it was Coleridge's letters—and read out a passage I'd underlined, something to the effect that small things work on a 'diseasedly retentive imagination.' He always imagines that I read just to find ways to unhinge him and I expected him to get angry. He asked me if I thought he had a 'diseasedly retentive imagination,' and I said I didn't know. I guess everyone does, at one time or another. He said he was worried about *me,* that he had a feeling something was going wrong for me. I said it had been a perfectly normal day. Then he went in the bathroom and ran the water for a while. He stayed in there for nearly an hour. I knocked on the door once and asked if he was O.K. He told me to go to bed.

"So I did. I must have been sleeping pretty deeply until about two o'clock, when I woke up and he was crouching over me. At first I thought he wanted to make love. But then I felt something wrapped around my head. It was the tape measure. It would have been funny, if I hadn't felt so confused. I asked him to explain what he was doing and he said he was measuring my head. And when I asked him why in the world he wanted to do that, he said he had been thinking about it and wanted to know if we didn't have the same *volume* in our heads."

"And do you?" I asked.

"I don't know," she said. "And I don't care." She paused. "I don't know what to think. On one hand I tell myself that he was honestly wondering about the volume of my head and only wanted to find out, that it was a problem, you see, that he'd set himself. It seems normal enough. On the other hand, I *know* that it is absolute madness to sneak up on someone when they're sleeping and take measurements of their skull."

"Why didn't he just ask you?"

"That's what we ended up arguing about. He says I'm suspicious of him and I think everything he does is some symptom of what I'm already convinced is wrong with him. I said that if he would just talk to me a little, about the sorts of things he's thinking about, I might be able to understand. I might be able to help him. I mean, most of the time I don't have any idea of what he's thinking about." She gave me a look of utter confusion. "I don't know what to think," she said. "What do you think?"

I didn't know what to think either, particularly in the light of my own strange meeting with her husband the day before. I didn't mention this to Maggie, for I feared it would only upset her further. She seemed to want me to pass some judgment on Richard, to tell her where she should draw the line. I explained only that I was unwilling to do that. She was annoyed, but when she had tried my determination with a few questions, she gave up and asked about my weekend.

"I went to Baton Rouge to see Clarissa Pendleton and I wound up in bed with a strange man."

"Why strange?"

"I mean a stranger. A man I don't know."

"Do you want to know him?"

"I'm not sure," I said. "I don't think so."

"Will he try to see you again?"

"I don't think so. I ran away from him."

"Oh?"

I finished my drink. "I don't even want to think about it," I said. "It hurts me to think about it."

"Why does it hurt?"

"Because I don't know why I did it. Why do I keep doing things like this? What is it? Am I sick?"

"Obsessed?"

"A diseasedly retentive imagination."

Maggie laughed. "It's interesting," she observed. "Your life is much more interesting than mine."

"I'm going to have another drink," I said.

"Did you tell Reed about this man?"

"Yes."

"What did he say?"

"He didn't say much. He was full of Nembutal."

"He doesn't mind?"

"Reed's not in a position to mind what I do, Maggie. He's at least as strung out as I am. And he knows it."

"Still . . ."

Maggie wanted to pursue it, but I couldn't bear to talk about it any more. I thought of Mr. Williams, of his nightmare life, and I was full of self-contempt again. I interrupted Maggie. "I talked to a man this morning, I mean I talked *at* him; he's only twenty-five, has some kind of nervous disease, his hands are like this . . ." I rattled my hands across the table, nearly upsetting my drink.

"Are you getting drunk?" Maggie asked.

"I just can't stand it," I said. "Why don't they just take a helicopter and drop those fucking stamps over the ghetto and let whoever's strong enough to get them get them. It would be fairer."

Maggie nodded sympathetically. "Did you hear about the poor madman?"

I said I had heard nothing of it. Maggie explained that another caseworker, Carolyn Boudreaux, had come to her desk and told her the story that morning. It seemed that six months earlier the man had been a client of Carolyn's, though she had spoken to him only once, in a regular intake interview. He had proved ineligible and, without much complaining, had gone his way. She hadn't thought of him again until she had received a call from the police. They said that a month after this interview, he had attacked a man who was twice his size in a bar. After a series of interviews with state psychiatrists, it was determined that he should be incarcerated. He had been committed to the asylum at Pineville, an infamous institution, where his behavior had degenerated considerably. The police told Carolyn that he had escaped, two weeks before, and traveled, walking, to New Orleans. He stopped in Algiers and murdered an old Negro woman whom he did not know, while she was sleeping. Then he disappeared for a few days. The woman's body was discovered by her nephew. She had been decapitated, but was otherwise untouched. Her head was not found. In the following week the police received four separate reports from residents in the uptown area. Each caller described answering a timid knock, to find a small, immensely excited black man standing on the doorstep, laughing hysterically, holding up a woman's head before him, his fingers knotted through the white hair. Before the shocked citizens were able to think of anything to do, the man turned and fled. The police had been unable to find him. Residents were warned to be on their guard.

"I would've thought you'd have heard about it from your neighbors," Maggie concluded.

"Don't they have any idea where he is?" I asked.

"They think he must be staying in town somewhere. Probably uptown. You know how easy it would be to disappear up there."

Maggie and I discussed what sort of life the man could be living. It was possible, I suggested, that he carried on fairly normally for days at a time. Then, mysteriously, the desire might come over him and he would take up his gory prize and go out again.

"It must be an irresistible temptation to know that you can do something so disturbing simply by knocking at any door," I observed.

Maggie seemed to find this idea distasteful. "I wonder where he keeps it," she said.

"He probably keeps it in a box somewhere. In his closet. By his shoes."

"He could bury it somewhere."

"Maybe he sleeps with it."

Maggie groaned. "Let's go," she said. "We're late already."

In my apartment that evening I found that I could think of nothing but the story Maggie had told me. Suppose the man came to my door. I felt certain that I would become hysterical if I opened the door and found him standing there. I tried to imagine the poor woman's head, after so many days of being carted around and displayed. What expression would she have on her face? Wouldn't her eyes be open and staring? And what condition would her skin be in? The more I thought about it, the more frightened I became. After I had eaten dinner I sat on my front porch until it was dark. Then I went inside and opened the front curtains. For nearly an hour I sat watching the street, thinking that if he came I would see him before he got to the door and I could run out the back way. Then I began to fear that he might come to the back door, as it offered a more accessible escape. I went into the back room and sat looking out the windows. It was ridiculous to think that he might come to my house, of all the houses uptown. And yet, I thought, he's probably hiding in the ghetto, just a block or so away. Why not my house? Wasn't it the obvious choice? Wasn't my burgeoning fear beginning to spread outside in a vapor that would be visible to his deranged sensibilities, directing him to my door?

When I could stand it no longer, I went into the kitchen and called Reed. His voice on the other end of the line steadied me. I told him the story and tried to joke about it.

"When did you hear about this?" he asked.

"This afternoon."

"And how long have you been worrying about it?"

"I know it's foolishness," I said. "I'm not really frightened, I just wanted to talk to someone besides myself about it."

I thought I heard a knock at the door and I nearly

screamed into the phone. Through this I could sense Reed's deliberation. "Reed," I said, trying to sound calm, "are you still there?"

"Look," he said. "I want you to do what I tell you and don't give me a lot of arguments."

"O.K. I won't argue."

"Good. Now go get all the clothes you need for a couple of days, whatever you need for work. And put on a record or something. I'll be there in a few minutes."

Relief washed over me. I thanked him, trying to think of some way to keep in contact with him until he was actually at the door. When I hung up I tried to do everything at once. I returned to the back room to prepare a few days' rations for my pigeons, all the while hoping that Reed wouldn't get distracted by something and take a long time in coming. A half hour would be the minimum, I thought. It would take him a few minutes to get started and he had to drive clear across town. I turned to the task of getting my clothes together. When I went into the bathroom for my toothbrush, I looked at myself in the mirror and laughed. What was I doing? Why had this fear gotten the better of me?

Ten minutes later I heard a car door slam and I ran to the front window, expecting to see one of the neighbors, or perhaps the little man himself, chauffeured to my door. Reed was halfway up the stairs by the time I got there and I realized, as I opened the door to him, that he must have run from his apartment and driven as fast as he could to get to me. I felt ashamed of having caused him so much trouble, but he was very solicitous and sensible, assuring me that I had done exactly the right thing to call him, chiding me for not thinking of him sooner. I allowed myself to be hurried about, questioned about having remembered my toothbrush, my "welfare shit," like a child going to camp. In the car my fear left me entirely and I tried to explain how exactly the thought of the man had taken hold of me. "It's normal," he said. "It could happen to anyone." He made me promise that I would stay at his apartment until the man was apprehended. I knew that was a sacrifice for him. He was something of a ladies' man and prized his solitude. Until that moment the strongest bond of our friendship had been our unspoken resolution that we would not, unless invited, disturb one another's privacy. I took his assurance as a compliment, seeing myself as I had been, trapped by my own imaginings, and as I was now, safe, befriended. I leaned back in my seat and rested my hand on his, blessing him inwardly, even as I marveled at his charity.

At Reed's apartment I took a long, hot shower and sat on the edge of the bed, wrapped in a towel, watching him shoot up morphine. The drug seemed to exhilarate him. "How does it feel?" I asked.

He smiled serenely. "Like my head is here, and I don't know where my body is. But I think you'll find me."

I laughed and stretched out on the bed. He sat gazing languidly into space, then turned to me, stroking my back and shoulders until I fell asleep. At midnight he awakened me to say that he had to go to work. I felt refreshed, and at his suggestion I got up, dressed, and accompanied him to the bar, a few doors down, on St. Philip.

The bar was full when we arrived, but by three o'clock it was nearly empty. I was playing chess with a friend of Reed's when Richard walked in. He didn't see me at first, but went straight to the bar, where he had two drinks in quick succession. He said a few words to Reed and, upon receiving his third drink, turned from the bar and surveyed the room. When he spotted me I nodded to him, uncertain whether to smile or look away. He raised his glass to me across the room, archly polite. So we would have another round. He came to my table and sat down, pretending to be interested in the game. I made two incredibly stupid moves before anyone spoke. My opponent looked up and asked, as he put my king in check, "What's come over you?"

Richard leaned over and whispered a move into my ear. I obeyed without thinking, aware only of the fact that he was frighteningly close to me and that he was drunk. Three moves later my opponent had my king surrounded and I gave up the game. Richard sat nodding as I threw the pieces dejectedly into the box, and when my opponent moved the set to the next table, where a challenger awaited him, Richard turned to me and asked what I was doing there.

"Losing the game," I said. "What about you?"

He put his fingers over his lips. "Couldn't sleep," he said. "Are you alone?"

"No." I pointed to Reed, who was watching us from behind the bar. "With him."

He laughed. "With Reed?"

"Why is that amusing?"

"Couldn't you resist *him?*" he said contemptuously.

I assumed that he was referring to Reed's reputation with women, and it annoyed me that Richard might think I didn't know about it. "I can resist you," I replied, getting up from the table.

He caught my hand as I pulled away. "Helene." He

whispered my name. I saw that he was pale, determined, and dangerously drunk.

"What do you want with me?"

"You didn't tell her, did you?" he said.

"No, did you?"

"Why don't you sit down here?"

I looked over my shoulder at Reed, who was talking to someone at the bar. "All right," I said, resuming my seat. "Did you tell her?"

"I can't remember." He said this seriously. "I don't think I did. I don't know why I would."

"How can you not remember something like that?"

"I think she knows."

"Knows what?" I said in exasperation.

"About us."

"You've had too much to drink."

He shook his head. "No. Haven't had enough yet." He finished his drink and pushed his chair back. "Do you want something?"

"Just beer. Tell Reed it's for me and you won't have to pay."

"I can pay," he said bitterly. He made his way to the bar and caught Reed's attention by holding his glass up over his head, as if he were raising his hand in school. Reed nodded to me as he pushed the drinks across the bar. After Richard returned to the table, Reed motioned for me to come to the bar. When I stood up, Richard caught my hand again. "Where are you going?"

"Reed wants me."

He pulled me toward him. "Don't go over there."

"Richard, please, don't make a scene. Besides, I want to go to the bathroom."

He dropped my hand. "I'm not going to make a scene," he said. "I don't care where you go."

Reed met me at the end of the bar. "Do you know that guy?" he asked.

"He's O.K.," I said.

"Why's he buying for you?"

"I don't know. I told him not to."

"Where do you know him from?"

"He's Maggie's husband."

Reed laughed and put his arm around my waist possessively. "How well do you know him?"

"Hardly at all. More than I'd like to."

He laughed again, now holding me by the shoulders at arm's length to get a better look at me. "You want him to go away?"

"No, it's O.K. I want to talk to him."

He drew me to him and kissed me. A man at the bar called his name out and another whistled in approval. "I like to have you here," he said as he released me. I looked at Richard, hoping that he had seen this little display, but he was looking into his drink. I went into the bathroom and stood with my back against the door. Why was my head spinning? It was true, I thought, I wanted to talk to him.

When I returned to the table, Richard sat looking into his drink.

"Do you come here a lot?" I asked weakly.

"Don't you know that guy is a junkie? He's a bum," he said.

"What difference does it make to you?"

"Did he even finish high school?"

"As a matter of fact, he didn't."

"Christ, what do you talk about with him?"

"It's not his conversation that attracts me to him," I said.

He raised his eyebrows, as if to say "Touché."

"Does Maggie know you're here?"

"Maggie's sleeping."

"Suppose she wakes up."

"She'll think I'm out walking."

"Oh."

"You want to take a walk with me?" he asked. "Get out of this smoke? We could walk to the Square."

"It's locked up."

"We could look through the bars."

"O.K.," I said.

Outside, Richard took my arm. I tried to ease myself free but he tightened his grip. "I need to hang on to you," he said. "I'm a little drunk."

We walked down Decatur toward the Square. It was warm and humid. The bums roused from their reveries as we passed and asked for small precise sums, fourteen cents, seven cents, enough to make up the price of cheap wine. We paid no attention to them and they didn't pursue us. At the Square we walked around to the front gate and peered inside. A police wagon stood open on the corner and a solitary drunk was being assisted inside by a patient policeman. This was a nightly ritual. Everybody in the van knew one another, the policeman knew them all. The last arrival mumbled to his companions as he took his seat and the policeman closed the door behind him.

Richard and I crossed to the alley and stood just off the street where we couldn't be seen. We heard the van start and drive away.

"I want to go into the church," Richard said.

"It's locked up."

"No," he said, "they never lock the side door. I go in there all the time."

We went to a door that opened into the alley, and to my surprise it was unlocked. We slipped into the cathedral and stood between a baptismal font and a row of burning candles.

"Are you Catholic?" Richard asked.

"No. But I went to Catholic schools."

"Me too."

He released my arm and I wandered farther inside. I stood in the nave and breathed the musty air under the high vaulted ceiling. Richard followed and stood hesitantly behind me.

"It's nice in here," I said.

He took my arm again and led me to the confessionals at the rear of the church. "I'm going in here," he said, lifting the curtain. "You confess to me." He disappeared inside, and I knelt down by the little window. I heard a tap and said, "Father, forgive me, for I have sinned."

"What are your sins?" Richard asked.

"Well, first, I've never been to confession before."

"You've never been in your life?" he said, sucking in his breath as if he were badly shocked.

"Also," I said, "I lie."

"About what?"

"About everything."

"And what else?"

"I'm disobedient."

"I knew it," he said. "And what else?"

"And I'm incapable of true contrition."

"That's bad," he said. "That's really bad."

"What can I do about it?"

"Don't worry about it. I can take care of it."

"How?"

His voice was low, mock-serious. "I'm going to beat it out of you."

We both began to giggle at this. The more I thought about myself kneeling there in the middle of the night, with this strange inebriated confessor ready to hear my sins, the more I laughed. Richard laughed too, as if he had never heard of anything so funny. He opened the curtain and we laughed at one another. I put my head in my hands and Richard leaned helplessly in the doorway of the confessional. Gradually I became aware of the silence that stood trembling at the edge of our laughter, and then I was laughing only to avoid that silence, full and hysterical, which stood around in the corners of the place, like pools of shadow ready to rush up the walls. We both stopped laughing, almost at once.

"Let's get out of here," Richard said. I sprang to my feet and we ran across the nave and out the side door. When we were in the alley he took my arm and we walked briskly toward Chartres.

"You felt it, too," Richard observed as we walked along.

"Christ, Richard," I said. "That was awful."

"It comes from me."

"What comes from you?" I asked incredulously.

"The power," he said.

"That's ridiculous."

He laughed. "Yes, you say that now. You're safe now. But it's true, and you knew it in there."

"You were afraid, too."

"I was only afraid of what I was about to do to you."

"You're imagining things."

As I said this he turned me into a parking lot and pushed me against a brick wall. "Don't move," he said hoarsely. I didn't feel afraid but obeyed him, thinking it best to humor him. I couldn't believe he was serious. He backed away from me, holding his arm out before him, pointing at me. "Don't move," he said.

I felt weak from my fear in the church, and confused by his behavior. I wished he wouldn't be so intense. I thought of Reed. I wanted to go back to his apartment and get some sleep. Richard continued to back away from me, pointing his finger as if to pin me against the wall. I could feel, pressing against me, his conviction that I couldn't move. Then, abruptly, he turned and fled.

I didn't follow him, but went back to the bar. When I walked in, Reed called out to me. I sat on a bar stool and watched him serve a customer before he came over.

"Where did you go?" he asked.

"I just took a walk," I said. "Over to the Square and back."

"With that guy?"

"His name's Richard."

Reed frowned. "I know his name."

"Does he come in here a lot?"

"About this time. A few times a week. He drinks a lot."

"What do you know about him?" I asked.

"You in love with him?"

I shook my head. Reed smiled and caressed me. "You look tired," he said.

"I think I'll go to bed."

"You're not scared any more?"

I pictured Richard's face as he fled. A feeling of absurd helplessness came over me. I laughed weakly. "Oh, Lord," I said.

"What is it?" Reed asked solicitously.

"I don't know. Just a rush. I think I'd better go to bed."

He put his hands on either side of my face and kissed my eyelids tenderly. Then he gave me the key to his apartment and, with one more kiss, released me from his warm influence. "I'll be at work by the time you get home," I said.

"Put the key in the mailbox," he said. "And call me later." As I walked out the door I paused, allowing the warm night air to sweep past me into the air-conditioned bar, feeling physical pleasure in the suspension of my body between the two qualities of air. On the street I thought of nothing but my destination, of safety and of sleep.

4

I stayed with Reed the rest of the week. Every morning we got up and searched the paper for news of the man with the head. "They probably won't say a word about it," Reed said, "until they catch him. They don't want to scare the public."

I called Clarissa that Friday and she offered to meet me at the bus station in Baton Rouge the following evening. Reed picked me up on Saturday and drove me to the station. "If she's not there," he said, "turn around and come back. I'll come get you."

I nodded.

"You're not just going up there to see that guy, what's his name, are you?" he asked.

"Michael?" I said. "If I see him I'll come right back, I swear it. He's the last person I want to see."

Reed kissed me and waved me into the bus. "I know you," he said.

Michael was, in fact, the first person I saw when I got off the bus in Baton Rouge. He was standing with his arm around Clarissa, looking uncomfortable amid the swarm of black people and L.S.U. sorority girls who poured out of the bus ahead of me. He was looking at the bus step, and when I was squarely on it, our eyes met. I pushed my hair out of my face, then swung down to the pavement, smiling to Clarissa, who, I saw at once, didn't suspect that I was walking toward more than I had bargained for. When I reached them, Michael took my bag deferentially and Clarissa introduced us. "Helene," she said, "this is Michael Pitt. You remember, I told you about him." She rested her hand on my shoulder and kissed my cheek. "Oh, I guess you don't remember," she concluded.

"I remember," I said. "He works late."

Clarissa laughed at this. Wasn't my memory amazing? she inquired of Michael, who expressed his admiration by pressing his lips into a dry smirk. "I hope you've forgiven me for last week," Clarissa said.

I looked at Michael, who was coolly appraising the pavement. His manner suggested that he was ready for anything.

"I've forgotten all about it," I said.

In the car, Michael paid close attention to his driving while Clarissa, sitting between us, chattered about their impending marriage. This was what she had wanted to tell me, she explained. She wanted me to see him, her future husband. The wedding would be small. The children were wild about their new father, excited about the idea of a wedding in their own house, in which they would participate. And would I be there? Would I come?

It startled me to see Clarissa carrying on like a girl, which she decidedly was not, and I was amazed to see that the years of awkward encounters and shattered affairs, the years that she had described to me as we sipped wine from crystal glasses (her last two; she had thrown the rest at her first husband when he asked her if she would be interested in sharing a bed with his mistress and himself)—I was amazed that she could have survived all this without having become cautious.

"Of course I'll come," I said. "Why wouldn't I?"

Michael gave me a curious look, then quickly returned his attention to the road.

"I guess I'm behaving foolishly," Clarissa said. "But I knew you would be happy for me. Not many people are."

"Why aren't they happy?"

"I don't know," she said. "I guess they're jealous. Or they don't think I'm fit to marry. Or they don't care. Happy people are never very popular."

"You deserve to be happy," I said. "And if you are, then I am too." She beamed at me, her hands unconsciously pulling her skirt down over her knees. She looked younger, more self-conscious, like a girl sitting between two adults, hoping they won't have an argument, hoping everything will go well from this minute on. I didn't envy her.

At the house we settled around the kitchen table, drinking wine and watching the children, who were playing with a dog on the back lawn. "Aren't you afraid they'll run into a snake?" I asked Clarissa.

"They don't come around the house much," she said. "I can't keep them from playing outdoors anyhow."

"There was one by the porch when I came, that night when you weren't here?"

"On the porch?" Clarissa inquired.

"No, in the grass. He went under the house."

Michael grinned at me over his glass. *"He* did?"

"A snake in the grass," said Clarissa, laughing.

"Are you afraid of snakes?" Michael asked.

"I don't mind them," I said. "But you can't tell which are poisonous and which aren't, around here. At least not until it's too late."

"That's true," he agreed.

"Are we talking about something else?" Clarissa asked, looking from Michael to me. I wondered how much she knew about him.

"Are we?" I said. "I hope not."

I was uncomfortable for the rest of the evening and tried to hide it by drinking a lot of wine and talking to the children. After dinner Clarissa took the younger off to bed and then agreed to take the older to a friend's house, where he would stay the night. "Mother wants me out of her hair," he informed me, leaning on the arm of my chair and helping himself to my wine.

Michael frowned at the boy. "It was your idea," he said. "You'd be bored here with us."

The boy considered this in silence. He gave me a look that indicated he was something less than wild about his prospective father. Michael told him to go and get his things together, and he left the room sulkily, without acknowledging the cheerful entrance of his mother.

"I won't be long," Clarissa said. "I'll just stop and pick up some more wine on the way back."

"Shall I go with you?" I asked hopefully.

"No," she said. "You two can get acquainted while I'm gone."

"Should I tell him about your checkered past?"

She laughed. "He already knows about that."

When she was gone we sat in cloudy silence. I filled my glass and tried to avoid the amused looks Michael gave me. After a few minutes of this, he leaned forward in his chair and put his glass down at his feet. "Why did you run away?" he asked.

"Why didn't you tell me?"

"Tell you what?"

"About this. About Clarissa."

"I thought you knew."

"I don't believe that."

"What difference does it make?"

"It makes a big difference."

"Not to me."

"Then I feel sorry for Clarissa."

"Oh really. Why don't you tell her, then?"

"I wish I could."

"You would have come home with me even if you had known."

"Can't we talk about something else?"

"Why did you run away?"

"You know why."

"Of course I do. But I want to hear your side of it."

I looked at him, wishing that I could avoid looking at him, wishing that I could keep from returning the knowing smile he gave me.

"Come over here," he said.

I sighed and put my face in my hands. When I looked up again he had not moved, but he was no longer smiling. He sat with his legs apart, his hands folded across his waist, looking at me seriously. He lifted his chin in a quick command as I stood up and crossed to him. He let me stand in front of him for a moment, so that we were both aware of my powerlessness, and then he pulled me onto his lap and began unbuttoning my blouse.

"Clarissa will be back soon," I protested, but I did nothing to suggest that I cared.

"I know," he said, caressing my breasts. "I'm not going to do anything." He kissed me, and again I felt him weaken, abruptly, involuntarily. Then he buttoned my blouse back up cursorily and suggested that we sit on the porch to wait for Clarissa. We didn't talk but sat drinking our wine in silence for perhaps fifteen minutes. When Clarissa arrived she asked him what we had talked about. He looked to me to give her an answer and I replied, without thinking, "We didn't talk."

In the morning I found Clarissa in the kitchen cooking breakfast. She gave me a cup of coffee and asked if I had slept well. I hadn't, but it seemed pointless to tell her. "All right," I said, looking out the window. "Where's Michael?"

"He's gone already. He had some kind of meeting."

"Oh." At the far end of the yard I could see a cat tearing at something in the grass.

"What do you think of him?" she asked.

"What's that cat doing?"

She joined me at the window. "It's a lizard, probably. They bring the dead bodies in here and put them in the kids' beds."

"Jesus," I said.

"What do you think of Michael?" she persisted.

I turned from the window and sat at the table. "He's very handsome. He looks like the sun."

She laughed. "Like the sun?"

"Like those pictures of the sun with the crooked smile and all the rays coming out like hair."

"Do you like him?"

"Does he like me?"

"He said he thought you were attractive."

"Did he say anything else?"

"Yes."

"Well."

She smiled as if she were ashamed to tell what he had observed. "And passive," she said. "Why didn't you talk to him?"

"He makes me nervous, to tell you the truth."

She laughed again. "He makes me nervous too."

"Why are you marrying him?"

"I think I'm in love with him."

"Clarissa," I said. "You once told me that was a bad reason to marry anyone."

She shrugged. "What else can I do?"

"Do you know why he wants to marry you?"

"No," she said. "I thought it might be . . . some kind of security thing. I don't know. He decided that we should marry really suddenly. I didn't think he was even considering the idea. He just said, one day, 'We'll get married.' And I said, 'Yes, we should.' "

"That's very romantic."

"You really don't like him?"

"I don't know him," I said. "If he makes you happy I'll learn to like him."

"I think you will," she said. "He's mysterious."

I didn't see Michael again that day. I felt dulled by my conversation with him, and it was difficult to spend the afternoon with Clarissa, who wanted to talk only of him. When he called to say he wouldn't join us for dinner, I was relieved. That evening Clarissa drove me to the bus station and I arrived in New Orleans a few hours later, determined not to see him again.

I called Reed. "I'm back," I said.

"Where are you?"

"At the station."

"Oh Christ. I can't come get you." His voice was drowsy, almost lisping.

"Is something wrong? Were you sleeping?"

"No," he said. "It's this dope I did. I can't drive, I'll wreck."

"I'll just go to my apartment."

"No," he said. "Don't go there. You have to come here."

"Are you sure you want me to?"

He sighed with impatience. "I've been waiting for you."

"All right," I said. "I'll take the bus."

"Great."

"Reed, what kind of dope?"

"Just reds. I got them this morning."

"I'll be there soon."

When I arrived he had left the door open and was lying on the couch. "Jesus, it's hot in here," he said. "Would you turn on the fan?"

The fan was a window contraption that drew in the air through a screen clotted with dead bugs. "You need an air conditioner," I said.

"I can't afford one. Anyway, I like to sweat." He fished in his pocket and brought out a plastic container full of bright-orange capsules. "You found your friend, this time? Up there?"

"Yes."

"You see that guy?"

"Yes."

"You saw him?"

"He's going to marry my friend."

Reed whistled. "Every time you go up there you get screwed and come home depressed."

"I know."

"I'm glad to see you, anyway." He stuck his index finger into the plastic vial and rolled up a capsule.

"I'm glad to see you."

"I almost wrecked this morning," he said. "I did some soapers, then I got these, and I did three. I got mixed up."

"How do you feel now?"

"I feel great. I don't know how I got home, though."

"You're not mixed up now."

He laughed. "I'm with you." He was having trouble talking and his eyes kept rolling up, as if they meant to slip away from him, slip back into his brain. "If I had a beer," he said, "it would be great. I would really be high."

"Do you want me to get you one?"

"I don't have any. I have wine."

"You want that?"

"That would be good," he said. The capsule had slipped back into the vial twice. He gave up, closed the top, and put it in his shirt pocket. "I'd like some wine."

I brought out the bottle and two glasses. He drank slowly, nodding over his glass. Then he slumped forward in his chair, his eyes closed. I sat down at his feet, watching the glass, waiting to catch it when the muscles in his hand relaxed. After a few moments he opened his eyes and smiled at me.

"Should you lie down?" I asked.

"No." He sat up and drank the rest of his wine. "I just

nodded out for a minute. I wish I had a million of these."
He put the glass down and drew me toward him, so that
I sat with my head resting in his lap. He pulled his
fingers through my hair. "Your hair is so thick," he said.
"What makes it so thick?" He pulled my hair, pulling
my face toward him, and kissed me languidly. "Let's go
in the other room," he said.

"Do you think you can?"

"In my condition?" He laughed. "I want to try."

In the bedroom he fell headlong across the bed, groan-
ing amiably. I climbed in after him and sat on the middle of his back. "I'm so down," he said. "You'll have to
be aggressive."

"I am aggressive," I said. I stretched out across his
back and began pulling at the laces of his shoes.

"I should have eaten," he said. "I haven't eaten anything today."

"Do you want me to fix you something?"

He rolled over, spilling me off his back. I clutched a
shoe to my breasts. "You are fixing me something." He
began working at his belt buckle. "How does this go?" he
mumbled.

"Are you all right?"

The buckle gave way beneath his fingers. He grinned,
flushed with success. "We'll see," he said.

Afterward he slept for an hour. I pulled myself out
from beneath him and sat on the edge of the bed, watching his face. His sleep was deep and dreamless. His eyes
didn't move beneath their lids; his breathing was barely
perceptible, slow, shallow, effortless. I was wide awake
and his sleep was a mystery to me. I lay down beside
him and touched his face with my own, so that I could
see nothing but his eyelids, behind which he was deep

in his sleep. When he woke I watched the struggle from this vantage. His eyes moved beneath the lids, once to the right, once upward, so that the lids were pulled open a little, then to the right again. A tremor started in his hand, moved up his arm, and culminated at his mouth, his upper lip pulling away from his teeth in a grimace, a wince. He was dreaming now, and through the dream he sensed my nearness to him. His eyes opened, blinked, opened wider, surprised to be looking into another pair of eyes. Something behind them registered my identity, clicked me into place. He wrapped his arms around my back and pulled me under him, hiding my eyes beneath the shadow of his shoulder. "I went to sleep," he said. "How long did I sleep?"

"A long time," I said.

He moaned. "I'm so hungry."

"I'll fix you something."

"No," he said. "Let's go out."

As we were walking out he pulled the pill bottle from his pocket, opened it, and regarded the contents affectionately. "Wait," he said. "I just want to take two of these."

"I'll drive," I said.

He swallowed the capsules and gave me the keys. "I want crawfish bisque. Let's go to Compania's."

The restaurant was crowded and we had to sit at the counter. Reed shifted about uncomfortably on his bar stool. "Look out for a table," he said. "I need something behind me."

"Are you sure you can eat?" I asked.

He smiled sheepishly. "I really feel great."

No table was to be had and by the time the food arrived, he was slumped forward peculiarly, his head

75

resting in his hands. His elbows kept slipping off the edge of the counter. Each time this happened he shook himself, pushed a little farther forward, planted his elbows firmly on the counter, and began sliding back again. His eyes had given up trying to focus. The waitress looked at me curiously. Should she leave the food? "Put it down," I said. "He's got to eat something soon."

He managed a few bites by himself, slowly, painfully; the distance his hand had to travel from the bowl to his mouth seemed to be continually doubling for him. The spoon missed the bowl, then traveled empty to his mouth, missed his mouth, smeared his cheek with brown juice, returned to the bowl, which it missed by several inches.

"Reed," I said, "we'd better go."

He shook his head, slowly, ponderously. The spoon was moving away from the bowl in my direction. I took it from him and stuck it into the steaming bisque. A kind of idiocy had begun to take possession of his face. Saliva gathered at the corner of his mouth. He reached up to wipe it away but his hand collided with his nose. His head dropped forward on his chest and the liquid streamed down his chin. "Reed," I said, "we've got to get out of here." I pulled a napkin from the holder and wiped his face carefully. The people around us pretended, with increasing difficulty, that they didn't see what was happening. The woman next to him had turned away, engrossed in the description the man next to her was giving of what was going on behind her back. Reed shook his head again and tried to take the spoon away from me. "Let me do it," I said. He dropped his hands into his lap. His face was so close to the bowl that I was able, for several minutes, to shovel the food into his mouth. He had difficulty swallowing and I was careful not to fill the spoon. I talked to him as I fed him, stopping every few bites to wipe the corner of his mouth, where an accumulation of brown saliva continually threatened to escape him. Each time I suggested that we leave, he shook his head and pointed to the bowl obstinately. I had the hallucination that people were making bets on whether I would be able to get the whole bowl of bisque down him and I was afraid to look away from him, afraid to see the money changing hands. Twice I tried to lie to him, to tell him that there was no more, but each time he nodded insistently at the bowl before him. His slump had become pronounced. He was aware of my discomfort and made hopeless attempts to set me at ease, pushing a cigarette in my direction, nodding his head in a circle that embraced the skepticism of the room, inclining his head to me as if he heard what I said. When the bowl was empty I stood up and tried to get my shoulder under his arm. "Let's go," I said. "Put your arm around me." The woman next to him looked at me with distaste. He slipped away from me and I stood behind him for a moment, puffing at my cigarette, trying to avoid the eyes that were gradually settling upon us from every table in the room. "Reed," I said, "try to help a little."

He pushed my hands away. "Leave me alone," he warned. "Get away from me." He straightened up, intending to leave. An expression of pleasant surprise crossed his face quickly, as if he had suddenly had a good idea, seen his way clear to something, found a solution. Then, as I pushed the empty bowl out of his way, he collapsed effortlessly, with sprawling grace, across the counter.

77

The woman next to him gathered in her purse and cigarettes and evacuated her seat. I sat down next to him. The waitress hurried over to us. "Did he take too many soapers?" she asked indulgently.

"I don't know," I said. "God knows what he took."

"You can leave him here a while. Maybe he'll come out of it."

"I can't leave him," I said. "If he comes out of it and doesn't know where he is, he's liable to get angry."

"Have you got a car?"

"Right outside," I said. "But he's so heavy."

She leaned over the counter and looked at Reed's face. "He's really out," she said. "He's getting kind of blue."

I wiped the corner of his mouth with a napkin again, stifling a desire to laugh. His eyes were slightly open, filmed over with stupefaction. "Reed," I said, leaning over him, "can you hear me at all?" But he was gone. His breathing was slow and regular. I pressed my fingers into his wrist, looking for a pulse. It was a useless gesture. I wouldn't have known a healthy pulse from an unhealthy one. The steady pumping of the blood beneath my fingers reassured me, and so I hung on to his wrist with one hand while I continued to wipe the spittle from the corner of his mouth with the other.

The waitress left me like this for a few moments, then returned with two young men who had been watching the scene from one of the tables. "Can we help you?" one of them inquired.

"I don't know where to take him," I said. "I guess I'd better get him to a hospital."

The taller of the two, a thin angular man with a foppish blond mustache, was leaning over Reed, pulling his eyelids open as if he hoped to find consciousness beneath them. The other informed me that he was a doctor at Tulane and that they would help me get Reed into my car, after which I could follow them to the infirmary. I agreed, and they began pulling him up from the bar stool by propping his arms over their shoulders. They made two attempts, the first one resulting in a noisy failure as Reed slipped away, smashing his head on the edge of the counter so roughly that I expected to see a rush of blood. The second time they pulled him straight back from the counter and dragged him, with some difficulty, down the aisle and out the door. I followed, keeping my eyes on Reed's feet. As I reached the end of the aisle, I heard one man complaining to another, "They ought to kill that bastard." I didn't stop to hear the reply.

Outside I hurried ahead of them, opening the car door and pulling the front seats forward. They had more trouble getting him into the car, as he was completely limp and kept slipping onto the floor. "Jesus, he's slobbering," the doctor exclaimed as a sudden stream of liquid ran from Reed's mouth onto his hands. "Do you know what he took?"

"Seconal," I said.

"How many?"

"I don't know. Five, maybe more."

"Anything else?"

"Soapers, earlier today."

"Anything else?"

"I don't know."

They settled him in the back seat, pulling his long legs up so that they could close the door. I stood outside the car with the doctor while his friend went to get their car. Then I followed them to the infirmary.

At the infirmary, in a display of concern over the emergency of Reed's condition, they left their car with the lights on and the doors open. I didn't follow but pulled the front seats forward and stood in the door looking at Reed. His mouth had gone suddenly dry, so dry that I could hear the slow rasping of his breath in his throat. His eyes had dropped open and rolled upward like a dead man's. There was a moment when the breath caught in his throat and I thought he was dying. I climbed into the back and pulled his head onto my lap. "Don't die," I whispered. "Reed, try to hear me. Don't die. You can't die." I was aware of lights going on inside the building, of the two men coming toward the car with a wheelchair between them, of the low hum of insects in the air, and of the perspiration on my hands and forehead. I thought, Now they're coming and it's too late because he's dead. Now they will try to take him away from me, but I won't let them. I thought I might just drive off quickly, drive around town with a corpse in my back seat, drive until someone stopped me. My hands were busy with something practical, transferring the plastic container of Seconal from his shirt pocket to the pocket of my jeans. In the process I found his heart beating beneath my hand. I had a vision of this heart, filled with blood, pumping the blood out, receiving new blood, pumping that out, oblivious to Reed, to me, to everything else except the necessity to keep pumping blood, to keep from drowning in blood. The two men arrived at the car and stood impatiently looking at me. I got out and watched as they pulled Reed from the back seat and settled him into the chair. His arms hung loosely over the sides, his chin nearly touched his breastbone, his legs dragged the ground. I pulled his feet into the footrest and followed the two men into the bright emergency room.

A nurse stood just inside the door, holding a clipboard and a pen. "Could you give me some information?" she asked me cheerfully. The men were hurrying Reed through double doors and I ignored her question, determined to follow them. I didn't want Reed out of my sight. She repeated her question, blocking me at the doors.

"I want to go with them," I said.

"You can go in a minute." She held out the clipboard with authority.

"All right. What is it?"

She clicked her pen, ready for action. "What's his name?"

"Reed."

"His last name?"

"Whitman."

"His address?"

"235 St. Philip."

"You wouldn't know his student number, would you?"

"He's not a student."

"He's not a student?"

"Is that all you need to know?"

She frowned. "If he's not a student, he can't come here."

"I'll go tell them," I said. The doctor came in, rolling up a blood-pressure mechanism.

"His pressure's O.K.," he said. "But he doesn't respond to anything."

"He's not a student," the nurse complained. "Why did you bring him here? You know he can't come here."

"Can I see him?" I asked.

He nodded, ignoring the flustered nurse. "I think we'll have to send him to a hospital to get intravenous medication. Do you have a doctor who can admit him anywhere?"

"No."

"Then we'll send him to Mercy."

The nurse went to call an ambulance, and I followed the doctor to a room where Reed lay on his back in a metal hospital bed. The other man was leaning over him, yelling in his ear. "Can you hear me? Hey. Wake up."

"What's his name?" the doctor asked me.

"Reed."

"Are you related to him?"

"No," I said. "He's my friend."

"You don't know what else he took? Just Seconal and soapers?"

"I don't know exactly."

"Reed," the other man yelled. "Reed. Wake up." He began trying to turn him onto his side. "He doesn't respond," he said. "He's really out."

I went to Reed and stood with my hand on his arm.

"He's your friend, huh?" the doctor said, as if the idea amused him.

Reed's face was peaceful, his hands were folded across his stomach. They had taken off his shoes and rolled up one shirt sleeve. I pushed his hair back from his face, wanting to kiss him back to consciousness, embarrassed to be wanting him so badly when he was so far from me and when my desire was a subject that would amuse these strangers. "Yes," I said, meeting the man's contemptuous smile.

"Some friend," he said.

The ambulance arrived a few minutes later. They moved Reed from the metal bed to a rolling stretcher and whisked him out of the room. I asked if I could go along, but everyone was in such a hurry I couldn't get an answer. I walked out to the ambulance and watched them push him inside. The doctor was talking to one of the attendants, telling him what Reed had taken and how long he had been unconscious. Then the doors closed and the blue light on the top began to spin and the siren blasted us all into silence as the ambulance pulled away.

"Has he ever done this before?" the doctor asked when we could hear again.

"Not like this. Not until he was unconscious."

"It's pretty stupid."

I realized how frightened I had been. My legs were so weak and my heartbeat was suddenly so loud that I thought I must be fainting. I could feel the blood rushing down from my head, draining down to hold up my knees. I waved my hand in front of my face, fanning weakly the warm, sticky, bug-infested air; taking one, two, deep breaths to hold on, to get some equilibrium.

The doctor watched me cautiously. "You could do better than that," he said. "A woman like you. Why would you want a man like that?"

"Where are they taking him?" I asked.

"Intensive care. Mercy. You can call in the morning."

I thought of the expression on Reed's face, just before he collapsed, and I tried to imitate it, to remember it more clearly. Oh yes, I thought. What a pleasure. Everything slipping away.

The doctor could disguise his growing contempt for my behavior no longer. "It's stupid," he was saying. "It's

a dumb thing to be doing, throwing your life away, trying to throw your life away. Do you think he cares about
you? If you hadn't been there, what would have happened to him?"

I came back to myself and I was annoyed at this man,
who whined at me through the night air like an insect,
like something that needed smashing. "Thanks for your
help," I said.

"It's my job."

"Then thanks for doing your job."

"You don't really care, do you? About what I said. Did
you even hear me?"

"I heard you," I said.

"I'm interested in you. I'd like to help you."

His friend, who had gone inside with the nurse, came
out and closed the doors of the car. When he started the
motor, the sound set me in motion like a cue. I headed
for Reed's car without acknowledging the man's com-
plaint. "You're running away," he called after me.
"You're running away."

❈ 5

I went back to Reed's. When I opened the door a big outdoor roach, confused by the light, ran headlong into the front of my sandals, smashing his soft forebody beneath my toes. I jumped back with a shout, kicking it loose so that it landed on its back, waving thin legs in the air. I took off my sandal and slapped it across the writhing insect, flinching at the crunch of its shell. Then I got a broom and swept it out the door.

It was hot in the apartment, but I didn't want to turn on the fan, because of the noise and because I dreaded running into another roach in the kitchen. I went to the phone and called the emergency room at the hospital. A nurse informed me that Reed was in the intensive-care ward, that he was still unconscious, and that they expected him to come out of it by morning. "But he'll have to stay another day," she said, "until we're sure he's strong enough to leave." I left the number and asked her to tell him as soon as he came to that I had called. Then I took a hot shower and lay in bed sweating until I fell asleep.

I called the hospital again in the morning. Reed had regained consciousness but was now sleeping, and the receptionist connected me with a doctor who greeted me with oily solicitude.

"Miss Thatcher?"

"Yes."

"Reed's going to be fine. He'll have to stay here today, but he'll be able to come home in the morning."

"What time?"

"First thing. At eight. Will you be coming to get him?"

"I guess so."

"Dr. Morrow from Tulane called last night. He was concerned about you."

"I know."

"You're all right?"

"Of course I'm all right. Reed's the one in the hospital."

"Yes." He was amused. "But we know how he is, because we've got him here."

"Can't I talk to him?"

"When he wakes up. I'll tell him you called."

"Tell him to call me at work."

"He knows the number?"

"Yes."

"I'll tell him."

"Thanks," I said, eager to hang up.

"Miss Thatcher?"

"Yes?"

"When Reed came to, he left a message for you. It doesn't make much sense. He was confused when he said it."

"What is it?"

"It may not mean anything."

"What is it?"

"He said to tell you that they caught the man with the head."

I laughed.

"Does that make any sense to you?"

"Yes," I said. "It does. Thanks a lot." I hung up before he could ask me what it meant.

Although I had nearly forgotten the man with the head, this news made me feel better. I went to fix some breakfast and found what I had failed to notice the night before, a newspaper folded open on the kitchen table. Reed had circled the article, on page 15, that told of the man's capture. They had found him across the river, about a block from the house of the woman he had killed. He was walking toward the house with the head of his victim in a shopping bag tucked inside his coat. I thought of him, pulling on a coat in the awful heat, convinced that such a disguise would render him unnoticeable. The article was short. The man's name was Isaac Freeman. He had been returned to Pineville. I read the article over and over while I ate a bowl of cereal and drank a half quart of orange juice. I wanted to talk to Reed, to tell him how relieved I was. I went to work feeling light-headed and cheerful for the first time in weeks.

I was early and was admitted by Clarence, the security guard. A few months before, one of the workers had been attacked on the stairs by an outraged client and Clarence had been hired to protect us on our expeditions to and from our desks. The first day he had come I overheard him laughing with two of the men workers about the good fortune of having a job that required him to stand at the bottom of a staircase and watch young women walking up. After eight, when we were all safe inside, he took his place at a desk just outside the receptionist's office, where he sat amiably, gun in holster, feet on desk, for the rest of the day. He was a light-skinned Negro, young, elaborately cheerful and polite. He knew many of the clients and greeted them, as they came in to be humiliated, with such charm and good will that they often hung about his desk for hours after their interviews, obscuring his view of those of us who were liable to be attacked. I was in the habit of meeting his eyes ten or twelve times a day, a quick exchange of looks in which he inquired if everything was O.K. and I telegraphed the message that, temporarily at least, I was safe. Since I rarely arrived at work early, and rarer still, in a good humor, he laughed and joked with me as he turned the key in the lock.

"Good morning to you, Miss Thatcher. You up early and smiling today."

"I just can't wait to get up there and start giving that money away," I said.

A small black woman who was leaning against the wall tittered over this remark. "I sure hope you my worker today," she said.

Clarence grinned. "You have a new boy friend, Miss Thatcher, making you silly this early?"

I winked and turned to the woman, to include her in this good humor. She smiled toothlessly, with hazy interest, turning her head so that I could see a partially healed knife wound that extended from just below her left eye to the corner of her mouth. I pictured her as she must have looked, pulling away from the advancing blade, a hopeless contortion of a face as she realized that she would fail to escape it. My laughter froze in my throat, and pretending to cough, I hurried past both of them and up the stairs.

Who did it to her? I thought. Did a man do it? Was it another woman? Was it her own child, her son? Did she go into his room and find him trying to raise a vein in his ankles or under his eyelids, searching for a vein that wasn't collapsed, and did she try to stop him, and did he pick up the knife that he always kept with him and lash out quickly at her, at his mother, because she was trying to get the syringe out of his hands?

It was no accident. I went to my desk to check on my first appointment, hoping that it wouldn't be this woman, that it would be a man and I would know I was safe. But it was a woman, Mrs. Esmeralda Hatchet. Now that would be too much. Mrs. Hatchet was thirty-five, had three children. The woman downstairs looked older than that. But it was probable that she looked older than she was. All these people did. Except the very old. Old people, seventy-five, eighty, older, often looked younger, preserved, thin, when they lived to be old. I went to the coffee pot and filled a paper cup. Maggie joined me there.

"You're early," she observed.

"For a change."

"Did you have a good weekend?"

"I can't tell any more."

"What happened?"

I told her about Reed.

"That's awful," she said.

"I wish that was all."

"What else?"

"You know that man I told you about, in Baton Rouge."

"Yes."

"He's marrying Clarissa."

"When?"

"Soon."

"Did you see him?"

"Uh-huh."

"Does Clarissa know?"

"No."

"Are you going to tell her?"

"I can't," I said. We walked past the long shelves of files, floor to ceiling, two rooms, to our desks.

"What about you?" I asked.

"Nothing much."

"Is Richard O.K.?"

"He spends hours in the bathroom. Hours. He locks himself in and runs the water. He doesn't take baths or anything. He just runs the water."

"How do you know he's not taking baths?"

"Well, he takes one in the morning. A shower. He doesn't like baths. Then he goes in later and runs the water. I can tell."

"Did you ask him what he's doing?"

"He says he's bathing."

"Did you tell him you didn't believe it?"

"He doesn't care what I believe. And that's what he says."

"Is he painting much?"

"Just this one big canvas. He's been working on it for weeks."

"What is it?"

"A bunch of figures falling past a city, down a big plastic chute."

"Sounds bad."

"That's what I thought at first. But people have painted worse. Subject matter doesn't indicate anything, that's what he says. Van Gogh painted flowers."

"You sound like a detective."

"I feel like a detective. If I knew what I was looking for, maybe I could find it."

"I know the feeling." We sat down at our desks and began shoving papers around and opening folders to prepare for the day ahead of us. Kay came by with two more stacks of folders, containing appointments that would come up in the next two weeks. I dropped mine into a drawer while Maggie looked through hers, checking the names at the top of each page.

"I keep expecting to find someone I know in these," she said. She finished the stack, then started over again. She didn't look well. It was not so much that she looked tired, though she did. There were dark circles under her eyes and her skin had an unhealthy pallor, splotchy and pale, almost translucent, over her forehead and cheekbones, stretched from lack of sleep. It was something in her manner, slower, painfully thorough, a change that had come about gradually in the last weeks, so that, sitting next to her day after day, I hadn't noticed it. As she tapped the folders against the desk to straighten them, her expression changed. Her teeth were clenched, her eyes were half closed, she was listening for something. She settled the folders into a basket and pulled her hair carefully behind her ears. Her nails were broken in places, not chewed but torn off. She saw me looking at her hands and quickly pulled them away.

"Should you stay with him?" I asked.

"I don't know what else to do."

"You could stay with me for a while."

"I can't just walk out on him. Even if I wanted to. Sometimes I think I'd better, for my own safety. But I can't believe he'd ever really hurt me." She paused, turning her hands up in her lap and examining her nails. "And there's something else."

"What?"

"I want to see what's going to happen. I want to watch him."

My phone rang. Maggie and I looked at each other. "Here we go," Maggie said, turning to her folders. I picked up the phone. "Miss Thatcher."

"How did I get here?" Reed asked sleepily.

"You passed out on me at Compania's. I didn't know what else to do."

"They won't let me go. I want to get out of here."

"I know. They said I could come get you in the morning."

"I have to stay here all night?"

"I'll come see you as soon as I get off."

"I hate it here."

"It's just for a day. You can get some sleep."

"I slept all night. I have to work tonight."

"I'll call Victor."

"No. I'll call him."

"Can I bring you anything?"

"Some soapers."

"Tell them you're nervous. Maybe they'll give you something."

"They gave me Valium."

"Did it help?"

He snorted. "One Valium?"

I laughed. "Just hang on. If you leave they might call the police or something and get you busted."

"I know," he moaned. "The food is awful here. It tastes like plastic."

"I'm sorry," I said. "I didn't know what else to do."

"You should have brought me home."

"Honey, you passed out on the floor. I had to get two guys to help me drag you out of the place. I could never have gotten you out of the car."

"Yeah. It's O.K. I guess I would have done the same thing."

"I'll be there as soon as I can."

"They told you about the man, huh? They caught him."

"Yeah. I guess I'll stay at my place tonight."

"What am I going to do all day here?"

"Look. I'll come at lunch. O.K.? I'll bring you the papers."

"Just bring me the sports page."

"O.K. I'll see you then."

He mumbled goodbye and hung up.

"Was that Reed?" Maggie asked.

I looked at the receiver. "He practically hung up on me. He's really mad."

"At you?"

"He wants to get out of the hospital. I put him there."

"That's ridiculous. What were you supposed to do?"

"I don't know. I guess I could have let him sleep it off in the car. But I was afraid he was going to die."

"He could have died."

"But he didn't."

Maggie scowled, then asked seriously, "Are you in love with him?"

"I try not to think about that."

"But why? How can you?"

"Because it would be pointless."

"I don't see why."

"What he understands is that I'm there. That's all he understands."

"And you're satisfied with that?"

"Maggie," I said, "do you love Richard?"

She thought it over. "I'm determined to. I have determined to. I said I would." She laughed. "In spite of him."

"That's what I mean."

"You think it's pointless."

"It's worse than that for you. It's dangerous. You know that. That's why you're so scared."

"I am scared."

"And so is he."

"Not as much as he should be. And *that's* what scares me."

"You think he doesn't know what's happening to him?"

"If he did, if he suspected, he would be more careful. He wouldn't want me to know."

"What *is* happening to him?"

"I can't be sure," she said. She looked at her hands, pulling them together so that her fingers interlaced. "I think he's losing his mind."

"You've got to do something."

She gave me a smile that chilled me. "Why?"

"Because he's taking you with him."

She shrugged, shrugging off me and my concern. "I wish that were true," she said.

The rest of the morning passed quietly enough. At lunch I went to the hospital to see Reed.

I found him sitting up in bed eating the spinach from his tray of food. "This is the only stuff I can stand," he said, holding up a long string of green for my inspection. He was wearing hospital pajamas that were too big for him, and when he stood up to escort me to the lounge, where we could smoke, he slipped his feet into what he clearly considered his greatest humiliation, brown paper slippers. They had shaved his right arm, a three-inch swath between his wrist and elbow, for intravenous medication. He kept plucking at his sleeve, pushing it up to look at the needle marks with an expression of fascination and shame. His eyes seemed to have sunk a few inches deeper into his head, surrounded by patches of gray chalky skin. He talked in nervous spasms, between which he looked at me vacantly, his lips pressed together in a tight line, curving down at both corners. "I'm restless," he said, lighting a cigarette and puffing at it impatiently. The look he gave me—baleful, full of a sickish glimmering—made me flinch. He was trying not to blame me, but he blamed me. "I might as well be in prison," he said.

"Reed, it's just for one day."

"Would you want to stay here all day?"

I looked around. The room was not unpleasant: white walls, government furniture, a television which was on. Two men sat in front of it, watching a quiz show. A boy, about eighteen, sat grinning at Reed like a friendly dog. Reed turned to him, smirking.

"What are you in for?" the boy asked.

"I overdosed," Reed said.

The boy nodded sympathetically.

"What about you?" Reed asked him.

"I'm getting my knee operated on. My kneecap got shattered."

"You going to be able to walk?"

"After the operation?" He smiled again, shyly. "I'll have a limp."

"Forever?"

"I guess so," the boy said. "You want to play cards?"

"Yeah." Reed gestured to me. "Later. When my girl leaves."

The boy looked delighted. "I'll go get my deck," he said, turning his wheelchair away from us.

"Jesus," Reed said when he was gone. "Poor kid."

"He likes you."

"Everybody likes me," he said. "The nurses hang around a lot. They think I'm funny."

"Then you'll be O.K. here?" I asked. "Until tomorrow. I'll come get you first thing."

He rubbed his forehead. "I wish I had some dope. I haven't been straight this long in years."

"How long?" I asked.

He gave me a mournful look. "Years. No shit. I don't know how long. It really makes me nervous."

"Will you be sick?"

"No. I don't think so. Just come get me first thing, O.K. And bring those reds."

"I'll be here," I promised. He walked me to the elevator.

As I walked through the glass doors of the hospital, I saw my reflection swinging past me, coming, then going and coming with me. I was self-conscious, walking across the marble landing to the stairs. I could see for a flash, a blinding revelation, like mindlessness, that was not far from simply blanking out altogether, fainting, how I looked. A woman, nearly thirty, small, tense, about to attack the step in front of her, about to decline to make that step, about to turn and run, about, always about to make a dangerous decision. I didn't feel, had never felt, that I was a beautiful woman. My face is ordinarily pleasant, my body is strong enough, healthy, not quite thin, but I knew, had always known, that I could have power over a certain kind of man if I wanted it. The power of weakness, the possibility that indecision hides a variety of strength. I knew that my manner on the street, in a chair, in a bed, particularly the last (I knew this), was to some men arresting, halting, not quite committed and hence (I had to ask myself) attractive. Or was it fatal? What I liked best was to be in transit, as I was then, to go from a lover to a lover, to a room, across a room, to close one door, moving to open another door, being in motion. Motion gave me all the beauty I might be said to possess. I felt this on the landing; the rest of the steps were an exquisite pain, like watching wings unfurl into flight, and then I was on the sidewalk.

I was late for my one o'clock appointment. Mr. Bodely had been waiting for twenty minutes when I opened the waiting-room door and called his name. He sat in the second row, and as he made his way past the knees of children and stolid women, I saw that he was going to be difficult. He was nervous, I could see that in the way his hands gripped the backs of the chairs and the quick looks he gave me, suspicious and severe. I introduced myself and escorted him from the waiting room. He was a small man, close to my own size, very black and prematurely bald. The lines in his scowling face didn't look as if they had been moved from their firm set for years. Clarence smiled at me over the man's head as we passed and I cast him what I hoped was a suitably helpless expression.

Mr. Bodely had never had food stamps before and insisted that he had not been able to work for several months because of an operation he had had on his foot. He couldn't explain how he had managed to live this long, and my efforts to get some kind of information I could verify made him more and more recalcitrant. He mumbled, he hedged, he repeated that he was disabled, that he could not work.

"I'll have to have a note from a doctor to that effect," I explained. "It has to be in the records here and it has to be signed by a doctor."

He began to paw inside the pockets of his worn jacket. "Looks like every time I go to that charity hospital they gives me a different doctor. I seen twenty doctors there. Which one's gonna write this note for me?"

"It doesn't matter which one. Any one. They all have access to your records."

"Now, one say I can work and one say I cain't."

"Then you must ask the one who says you can't."

"But you don't get to see no doctor there just 'cause you wants to see him. You has to see the doctor they gives you."

"Then go until you get the one you want."

"Miss, I can tell you I cain't work, not with my foot like it be. How can I work after this operation?"

"When was the operation?"

"It was in the winter."

"And you still can't work? You aren't better yet?"

"Now it's in my toe, the damage been done and there ain't no way to repair it. I ain't going to be able to work again for a long time with this here damage."

"But how have you been living since this operation? Where did you get money to live?"

His hand stopped inside his coat pocket and he leaned forward to repeat what he had told me three times before. "I ain't been doing no living, miss, not that you could call it that. Some folks go downtown and they get in a lot of trouble and they rough, you know, these young boys. But sometimes I gets a quarter and sometimes a dime, here and there, and my brother he give me a dollar now and then, but that's all I got, because this here damage has been done, and some folks in town get into a lot of trouble because they keep going down there. They will insist, they's got to go down there. But this ain't hardly living, not with the damage that's been done here."

I looked at the form in front of me and tried to think of a question that he wouldn't be able to evade. When I looked up he produced something from his pocket and set it carefully down on the table between us. It was small, crusty, and brown. At first I thought it was a date. I glanced at it, returned my eyes to my form, and then realized that I had seen, at one end of the date, the pale inset of a nail. I looked at Mr. Bodely, who was mysteriously calm. "Is that your toe?" I asked.

His hand slid out across the table and closed over the toe.

"The damage been done," he said calmly. "There ain't no way to repair this kind of damage to a man."

"Mr. Bodely," I said, surprised to hear that my voice sounded more amused than enraged, "lots of people don't have their toes or their fingers or even their eyes, but they make a living. They can explain how they make a living."

He pulled his coat closed and pushed his chair back

from the table. "Miss, you don't understand nothin' about nothin' and that's a fact." He stood up.

"If you can explain how you've been living for the last four months I might be able to help you. I can't do anything unless you're willing to tell me that."

"And what could you do if you knew?" he asked, standing over me. "What do you think you could do?" He turned away before I could answer and left me sitting at the table with my charts and forms spread out before me.

As I passed the waiting room on my way to my desk, I saw Mr. Bodely talking animatedly with the receptionist. I hurried by, hoping that he wouldn't see me, turn on me, point at me in the hall.

"You look upset," Maggie observed as I sank gratefully into my chair.

"A man just threw his amputated toe on the table in front of me."

She grimaced. "What?"

"He had his toe, it was all pickled or something, and he put it on the table."

"Why?"

"To prove he was disabled."

She laughed. "Are you serious?"

"It's true. He's out there now, talking to Kay. He probably wants to tell my supervisor I cheated him."

"His toe? Which one?"

"I don't know. I didn't get a real good look at it."

"His big toe?"

"No, it wasn't his big toe."

"I've got to see this," Maggie said. She went to the reception door and looked out. I could see Mr. Bodely, closing in on the impervious Kay, while a small Negro woman complained behind him. He had broken into the line.

In a few minutes everyone in the office knew about Mr. Bodely. Mr. Jackson, a new black worker who sat across the aisle, informed me that some voodoo process had undoubtedly been set into motion when the toe was placed on the table before me.

"Will my feet rot?" I asked him.

"Don't see him again," Mr. Jackson suggested. "Let your supervisor handle it. If he would try something like that, he must be desperate."

"He's crazy," I said. "But what doctor would give him his toe to keep?"

"It may not be his."

"I'm not going to think about that," I said.

Mr. Jackson smiled. "You'd do best to forget the whole thing."

But I couldn't take his advice. I had to tell the story over and over for the rest of the day. Everyone wanted to hear it. I wrote a detailed account of the interview and sent it to my supervisor. In the space for the rejection code I put "26: failure to explain management."

By the time I got home that evening, the incident seemed more amusing than ominous. I wasn't thinking of Mr. Bodely, I wasn't thinking of anything at all, when I opened the door and saw an envelope on the floor. I thought it might be a note from Reed, saying that he was discharged from the hospital, had gone home on his own. It didn't occur to me that this would have been an unlikely means of notifying me until I turned the envelope over and saw my name in red ink scrawled across the front. I thought of Mr. Bodely, and then I thought of Michael. I stood in the doorway holding the envelope and for a moment I couldn't move, couldn't begin to open it. Who would write my name like this, scrawl my name impatiently on an envelope and slide it under my door so that I would find it there and stand there, in the doorway, holding it, reading my name, afraid to open it? I turned to look out at the street; perhaps the sender was watching me, watching to see how I would react to what I would find inside. The street was empty; an old woman sat placidly on her porch across the way. I closed the door and went to the back of the house, holding the envelope.

I put the letter on the table and fixed a cup of coffee. It was Michael, I convinced myself. He would do something like that, passing through town, leave a note under my door, a note which would be noncommittal. He would want me to meet him somewhere, a hotel or a restaurant. I knew I would go.

I looked at the envelope again. His handwriting wouldn't look like this. He would write my name with calm deliberation, or he wouldn't write it at all. I opened the envelope and took out a half piece of legal paper. It read, in the same frantic script, "Helene, this is it. Tonight, the cathedral, midnight." At the bottom of the page there was a convoluted but identifiable *R*.

Reed? No, Richard. I should have known. Maggie was right to be afraid for him, I could see that in the shape of the letter he used to identify himself. And what made him think I would meet him in the middle of the night, for what purpose? Would he attack me, was that what he meant? But I thought this unlikely. Whatever Richard wanted from me, he wasn't mad enough to try to force me to it. What he wanted, I thought, was my consent. And would he get it? I laughed, put the note in its envelope, and threw it on the table. It annoyed me to have this unlikely decision forced on me, but at the same time I was amused, delighted. I sat at the table for a long time, eating dinner, watching my pigeons come into their coop and settle down for the evening, reading Richard's note over and over, pruning my plants and planting pieces in dark rich potting soil, setting them out in new red clay pots. In this way I busied myself until eleven, pleased with myself for being so industrious, enjoying the quiet of my apartment. I took a long, hot bath, dressed in jeans and a shirt, put on my sandals at the door, and walked to the streetcar stop a few blocks from my house. The street was well lit, there was no one around. I was the only one on the car all the way down St. Charles. At Canal I turned onto Bourbon, always a busy street, bright and full of people at any hour. Now and then a man would approach me, talk to me, try to draw me into one of the bars, but I made excuses and thanked them so sincerely that they let me go on, calling after me for a phone number, an address. "Anything," one drunken young man entreated me for nearly a block. "Give me anything." I unscrewed one of my earrings and pressed it into his outstretched hand. He looked at the token dazedly, then, as if he saw in it something of immense value, closed his other hand over it and staggered away, holding his cupped hands before him like a man in prayer. All this amused me, the relentless and often helpless oppression of men that this street represented; this amused me, like a slave who knows his master can't understand the language of slaves and has no power in that language, I had a certain indestructible freedom. There were other women around: prostitutes leaning listlessly against the walls;

wives hanging on the arms of their husbands in the hopes of saving them from the cool hands of the prostitutes; young women on dates, giggling, wide-eyed as the doors to strip shows flew open before them and they saw themselves in the dead eyes of the slowly gyrating women on the runways; an occasional woman alone, but this was rare, moving quickly, as I moved, down the crowded street with a destination in mind. I felt myself in the eyes of all these women, willing, patient, curious, more alive than any of the men who had to ask themselves, when they got home, what they had hoped to find on that street. I found it, walking on the street, moving through a maze of eyes. It was being vulnerable, a woman, safe in motion, likely to be stopped. I crossed Royal at St. Peter and walked through the alley to the cathedral. There were a few people about: a policeman stood on the corner, a couple sat on the step to the square, another couple disappeared around a corner. I tried the side door to the cathedral, found it open, and slipped inside. I expected to find Richard waiting for me, but the church was empty.

At least it looked empty. As soon as the door closed behind me, I began to feel that Richard had planned something unpleasant for me. I went into the nave and stood by the baptismal font. It was dark in the church and terrifically quiet; the sound of my own footsteps disturbed me so much I stopped and took off my sandals. There were candles burning in the back of the church and two more racks in the front, just before the chancel, but the center of the nave was dark. I thought I saw someone move behind a plaster saint that stood at the base of the pulpit. It would be Richard, I thought, trying to frighten me. What pleasure did he get from that? I wanted to call his name but couldn't bring myself to break the heavy silence. If he jumps out at me, I'll shout, I thought. I clenched my teeth and bent my knees so that I would be able to move quickly and quietly. I would be out the door before he could get anywhere near me. Unless he was right behind me. I looked over my shoulder and saw the confessional. Of course, he would wait in there. I passed the curtained window and looked inside. It was empty. I decided to sit in the last pew and wait for him. If anyone came in, I wouldn't be noticed. I imagined that the sexton must be around somewhere, that he might come into the church to make sure no one was carrying off the altar cloths or writing obscenities on the sacristy. I looked around at the statues of saints, the drawings of golden angels, the flickering candles. I remembered that there was a grave in the front of the church, the grave of Don Almonester, a builder of the city, who existed in my imagination only as the grandfather of the Baroness Pontalba. I thought of the baroness, a big ugly woman, German and French, I imagined. I had seen pictures of her and knew the story of how her father-in-law tried to kill her with a shotgun. She had tried to protect herself with her hands, which were peppered with shot. The shot was never removed, and as an old woman, she lost control of her hands, so that they jerked about uncontrollably, a phenomenon her children referred to as "Mamma's bullets." I thought about what her life must have been like in the colonial city, a swamp of a place, plagued by fires and insects, probably alligators and snakes, animals the baroness would not have been likely to know from her native country. She had outlived the man who tried to kill her; he shot himself shortly after. I didn't know why he had tried to kill her. It occurred to me that I should try to find out. I went to the front of the church and looked at her grandfather's grave. Did she visit this grave? What had the city meant to her? Did she wish to die here? As I stood there, thinking of her, I decided that whatever Richard had in mind I wouldn't wait around for it any longer. I left Don Almonester and the cathedral that was his tomb and went out into the alley.

❧ *6*

I saw Richard as soon as I opened the door. He was standing at the end of the alley, leaning against the wall of the cathedral. I turned away from him and walked to Chartres. I could hear him behind me, following me. It was absurd. I knew he was following me and he knew I knew, but neither of us spoke. He stayed a half block behind me. I considered taking a streetcar home, but that meant walking all the way back to Canal and then waiting, perhaps for an hour. If I had to stand on the corner with Richard watching me from some post nearby, I doubted whether I would be able to keep my resolve not to talk to him. The situation annoyed and pleased me all at once. I felt curiously safe, knowing he was behind me. I didn't have to look back to see if he was there. I walked up Chartres to St. Philip, then to Decatur, where I knew I could find a cab. The air was fluid and warm around me, and I felt as if I were moving through a dream landscape. There were people around me, brushing past me without seeing me. When I got to Decatur, there was a cab standing at the curb, the motor running, waiting for me. I got in and gave the driver my address. As we pulled away from the curb, I rolled down my window and looked out just in time to see Richard turning away. What a madman, I thought.

There was little traffic. I was driven through the dark-ened city rapidly and quietly. My head had begun to ache. I was thinking of Maggie. Shouldn't I tell her? Her husband sent me notes, he followed me on the street. How could I tell her? And why was he doing it? When we arrived at my apartment I gave the driver a large tip, for which he thanked me by waiting at the curb until he was sure I was safe inside. I went from room to room turning on lights. I had decided to write Richard a letter. I made a cup of coffee and sat down at the kitchen table with paper and pen. I wrote:

Richard,

This is ridiculous. What do you want from me? There's noth-ing I can do for you, you must know that.

I saw you tonight when I came out of the cathedral. Why were you following me? Why did you ask me to come there? Believe me, I thought twice about going. But I thought you might need to talk. You must talk to someone. That was the only reason I came.

Maggie is worried about you. Have you looked at her lately? Why are you treating her so badly? She would help you. She would be more likely than me to help you.

You must know that you need someone to help you, other-wise why follow me around?

I was afraid to talk to you.

Please leave me alone. Don't send me any more messages, don't follow me. I'm frightened of you. You don't know any-thing about me, though you may think you do. I have enough trouble without you following me around. Please stop. Leave me alone.

I read over what I had written. How would I deliver it? And wouldn't this be precisely what he wanted, for me to beg him to stop? It wouldn't work. I crumpled up the page and started another letter. When I began, I didn't know who I was writing to. Gradually it became clear to me.

Here's a letter. I knew I would wind up writing one. Why did you have to make me write one? Would you be surprised to hear that I don't understand what you are doing? I search and search, I make up reasons, excuses for you. I am trying to see what you have in mind for me. I can't believe you have nothing in mind for me. If that were true, why bother?

Why bother even once?

It confuses me to be impatient. I am not usually impatient. It's something about you. Something to do with you.

What makes you think I won't require some explanation for this kind of treatment? I wouldn't treat a dog this way.

Where are you? Are you in your office working on your book? Do you think that book is important?

Why did you act as if you wanted me if you really didn't? Why waste your time?

Or was I not right? Was I something you didn't expect? Not right? Was it that obvious?

Are you sparing me something? Please don't spare me. If I don't know what's really going on with you, it's not because I don't want to. Why are you so secretive?

Do you think I think I need to be saved? That you could save me? I don't care about that. I'd be saved if I knew what was going on.

I don't mind being used, if it's to some purpose. But I have never been used this badly. I can't help it.

How are you doing this? Are you telling yourself you regret the whole thing? Are you wishing you didn't have to think about me?

Are you thinking about me?

I read this over. I felt sorry for myself, reading it. Sad, I thought, to sit down and deliver yourself of something like this. What miserable woman had written it? I hadn't even known what was on my own mind, a secret I was keeping from myself. Here it was. It wasn't like me to feel this way, to be hurt by someone else's neglect of me. Why should Michael explain himself, what had happened between us? How could he? He might understand less than I.

But I understood nothing. I rested my elbows on the table and rubbed my eyes with my fingers. I told myself, Forget it, it's not in your power, go to bed, go to sleep. I turned out the lights and set my alarm so that I would have time to meet Reed at the hospital in the morning.

I got up at six and spent some time leaning over the sink in the bathroom, trying to cover the circles under my eyes with makeup. I examined the lines around my mouth, across my forehead. I covered the lines with powder, then wiped it away. I practiced different expressions—annoyance, determination, delight—but through each one only weariness showed. A tired woman. I didn't look forward to dragging myself through the day.

The phone rang at seven-fifteen, just as I was going out the door. I ran to catch it, picked it up doggedly, gave my indifferent hello.

"Helene," Reed said. "This is me. Don't forget me, for Christ's sake."

I laughed. "I'm on my way."

"Great. Just a few more minutes in this place. Don't forget my reds."

"They're in my purse," I said.

"Soon they'll be in my mouth."

"Did you sleep O.K.?"

"No. I didn't sleep. I called you but you weren't home."

"I'll tell you about that when I get there," I said.

As I was driving to the hospital, I began to feel ill. My head was throbbing so violently I pressed my forefinger against my temple to see if the skin weren't being lifted. My stomach was weak, fluttery, rumbling about in its emptiness. I was salivating heavily, swallowing continually and with difficulty. I found a parking spot in front of the hospital and went inside without putting any money in the meter.

Reed was leaning over the check-out desk, pretending to be interested in the questions the nurse put to him. I walked up and stood beside him before he saw me. He acknowledged me by putting his arm around me and kissing my throbbing temple. The nurse looked at me cheerfully. "She's taking me home," Reed told her. "She won't let me kill myself. You can sleep tonight."

The nurse showed her distress at his levity. "You could have died," she said. "Don't you care?"

He signed the page she turned out on the counter. "If I had to stay here another minute," he said, "I might as well die."

The nurse signed her own name under Reed's. "I'm sorry you think it's all such a joke, Mr. Whitman."

Reed glanced at her name, then turned away from the counter. "It is a joke, Shirley," he said. I followed him to the elevator.

Outside, he sprinted down the steps to the car and threw the door open for me to get in.

"You're a free man," I observed.

111

"Sure," he said skeptically.

On the drive to the office I told him about my adventure of the night before.

"I don't want to scare you," he said when I had finished, "but I think that guy is dangerous."

"I don't think he would hurt me."

"You never think anyone would hurt you."

"No one has," I said.

"You got my reds?"

"They're right here." I opened my purse and gave him the bottle of pills. He took two and gulped them down.

"Actually," I said. "I think everyone would hurt me."

"Do you think I would?"

"If you had to. Yes. I think you would."

"I wouldn't."

"You wouldn't have to. I'm not in your way."

"I was depressed last night. I couldn't sleep. I thought about you and me. I thought you were different than other women to me."

"You were straight."

He grinned. "Sure. I don't want to talk about this, either."

"It's not that," I said.

"You went to school a lot. I know it's hard for you to talk to me. I didn't spend much time in school. I didn't listen to anything when I was there. I thought about going back. But it's too much trouble."

"I didn't learn anything in school," I said. "I learned a lot of trash."

"When we go to those films you like, you always get a lot out of them. You know what they're about. I don't know that stuff."

"All that means is I'm stuck in one way of looking at

them, which makes it impossible for me to enjoy them. Like you do. You enjoy them. You like to go as much as I do."

He considered this. "I like them," he said. "That's true."

"You don't have to understand something to get pleasure from it," I said. "Sometimes it's better if you don't."

"I don't understand you," he said, running his hand along my thigh. "But I get pleasure from you."

"I know," I said. "I'm in the same condition."

"We're friends," he concluded. He stretched his legs out and rested his face against the car window disconsolately.

"It was that bad, huh?" I asked.

"No," he said. "I could stand it. I just wish these reds would hit."

By the time we arrived at the office, he seemed to feel better. As I was getting out he stopped me. "Has that guy Richard ever told you that shit about the shape of his mind?"

"The what?"

"The shape of his mind. The inside of his head. He's got a thing about it. He goes on about it after he's had a few drinks. I listened to him for a long time one night, just because there wasn't anything else to do. It's not just a drunk man babbling. It's a sickness with him. I think he's crazy."

"Poor Maggie," I said.

"Poor you. I don't like that guy writing you notes and following you around. The next time he does it, you ought to call the cops. Or call me."

"I will," I said.

He laughed. "You might."

We kissed briefly and parted. Inside, the office was already crowded and I hurried past the waiting room to sign in fifteen minutes late. My supervisor stood in the door of her office, her impatience at my continued tardiness barely concealed. "There's a note for you on your desk," she said. "Your ten-thirty wants to reschedule."

I nodded and turned away.

I gulped down a cup of coffee and called the receptionist to see if anyone was waiting. "Your eight-thirty," Kay said. "Is Maggie there yet?"

Maggie's desk was in a state of unusual confusion. Her chair was pulled out and her purse hung over the arm, half opened, as if it had been thrown there. "She's in," I said, "but she's not at her desk."

"Would you tell her J. Fedora is here?"

I scribbled the name on a pad and set it on top of a stack of cases on her desk. As I went through the door to the reception room, I saw Maggie coming in with a cup of coffee in one hand and a case record in the other. She nodded to me and I waved.

My eight-thirty was Willie Mae Hudson, and her application said she was ninety-two years old. The woman who answered to this name didn't look that old. She walked with a cane, bent forward at the waist. Her face was lined, the brown skin stretched tightly over high cheekbones, a face that must once have been remarkably beautiful, now hawklike and determined, the eyes miraculously youthful, bright and unclouded. She followed me to the interviewing room without speaking and placed her cane in the corner, seating herself without difficulty.

I introduced myself and determined that she had been

114

receiving food stamps for some time and knew what was expected of her. I turned to the application.

"Is this your correct birth date?" I asked.

"Tha's right. I be ninety-two.'"

"You don't look it."

"I don't feels it, honey. I feels younger than ever, but still closer to the Lord than I was, so it be a good feeling."

"You live by yourself?"

"There's no one else living in my house if tha's what's worryin' you. 'Cept I got me an old dog I've had these last twelve years and he's my companion. He waitin' on me to go, to see me out, and I'm waitin' on him, so he won't go without me, so I reckon we be dying together." She drew in her breath raspingly and appraised me to see if I would let her go on or if I was in a hurry. I put my pen down and looked into her dark eyes. "Every person you meet be someone," she continued, "and every li'l thing you see is something to see. If a chile like you can see that, then the world comes sweet for you and you thankin' the Lord for every day what He gives you, every breath what He breathes into your mouth. But no children can see much these days, they busy lookin' round for a way to keep from seein' the love of the Lord. And I don't know why they doin' that, wastin' the life the Lord loves in them. Does you know why they does that?"

"I don't know," I said.

"Now my gran'son, he like that. He come visitin' me and he cain't wait to get hisself out the door an' into some trouble what's waitin' for him out in the street. He don' like to be aroun' me 'cause of my oldness, and my closeness to the Lord what he can feel when he puts his big shiny shoe on my front porch. Now he's a grown

115

man what should be making his peace with the Lord beginnin' today, right now, but he thinks he be smart puttin' off the Lord, pretendin' the love of the Lord ain't the only thing what keeps his soul from flyin' right out of his body and into the hands of the devil."

I was silent. I hoped she wouldn't stop talking in this way.

"You can only put off the Lord so long, then you cain't put Him off no longer. Now this boy Samuel livin' in danger of losin' his life, a young man like that, an' losin' it without ever havin' no pleasure in his life, no love for the Lord or for the ignorant people what's takin' advantage of his uselessness, and for the poor people what he takes advantage of. He think it be important to get ahead in the world, and tha's the only thing I ever tole him, when he was sayin' how he had to go and try to get ahead in the world, I said, 'Samuel, the way to get ahead in the world is to love your own life and praise the Lord you got a life to love.' But he think I'm just a crazy ol' woman babbling on with no sense in me. So I prays for that boy every morning an' every night. I prays he gonna see before he die, I prays for the Lord to open his eyes." She chuckled to herself. "Prayin' for that chile keepin' me alive. I don' believe the Lord gonna take me back with Him till we finds a way to save that boy between us." She closed her eyes and smiled, leaning forward in her chair and folding her knotty brown hands in her lap.

"Mrs. Hudson?" I said after a moment.

She opened her eyes and looked into mine confusedly. Then she pulled her purse open in her lap and searched among the contents. "I be forgettin' you gots your job to do," she apologized. "I brung all my papers whats I bring every time. I got my Social Secur'ty here, and my rent paper. Here's all these papers." She pulled out three envelopes and spread them across the table. "They don' mean a thing to me," she said. "They's just papers. But I knows you needs 'em for pictures."

"Yes, ma'am," I said. "I'll go make a copy of them. I'll be right back."

When I returned she was sitting with her hands folded in her lap, her head bent over her chest. She shook herself as I came in, then gave me her attention as I explained what she would have to do to purchase her food stamps and how long it would take. She nodded her head vigorously at each sentence, to show that she understood what was required of her. We concluded the interview and I stood up to escort her to the door. As we walked down the hall, she said, "I'm movin' too slow for you. I wish I could go faster."

"You go fast enough," I said. "I hope I move as fast as you when I'm your age."

She laughed. "The Lord will keep you movin'," she said. "Now I been talkin' to you and I see you good, you is a listener. And the Lord will let you live a long, long time. You be as old as me."

"I hope so," I said.

"That shows sense. Some people don't want no long life. But they's scared to die, just the same."

We arrived at the door. Mrs. Hudson put her hand out to me and I took it in my own gratefully. I felt that her touch filled me with strength, with her pleasure in life. I wanted to go out the door with her. She released my hand and turned from me, leaving me excited. By the time I got to my desk I felt impatient and alone, convinced that I would not be like her and ashamed of myself for pretending, even for a moment, that I might.

I tossed her application on my desk and sat down in a huff.

"Trouble already?" Maggie inquired.

"No," I said. "Just an old woman, poor as a mouse and happy as if she were rich."

"And that makes you mad?"

"When I was in high school, the nuns used to say that the soul was like a container of grace, everybody could fill their container, but some people, like saints, had great big containers and others had little ones. I think mine's a thimble."

Maggie laughed. "That's ridiculous."

"Isn't it?" I said. "They were always saying things that didn't explain anything."

"Do you believe in grace?" she asked.

"Only when I run right into it."

"Then you do believe in it?" Her voice suggested that she was more than intellectually interested in my answer. I caught in her expression the hysterical expectancy that comes with exhaustion. As I became aware of this, she turned quickly away, her face flushed with embarrassment.

"What is it, Maggie?" I asked carefully. "Are you sleeping at all?"

"I sleep all right," she said coolly.

"I don't want to pry if you don't want me to. But I can see you're wearing yourself out about something. If it would help to tell me . . . or if it would help to tell me to mind my own business. I don't know."

She smiled weakly. "I'll tell you soon. As soon as I can, as soon as I know myself."

"All right, then," I said, determined not to push her to an untimely confession.

The rest of the morning passed quietly. Maggie and I were in and away from our desks, busy with clients and cases, and we didn't try to talk again. In the afternoon she stretched her arms out across her desk and fell asleep for a few minutes. When she woke up she said she had a headache and decided to go home for the rest of the day. After she had gone I gave my attention to Mrs. Hudson's case record, which was an orderly one, unembellished by the frustrated comments one often found in cases that had been in existence for any duration. As I was completing the last form for her certification, the phone rang.

I picked it up and said my name, still penciling in the last three digits of Mrs. Hudson's Social Security number.

"Helene?"

I didn't recognize the voice. "Yes?" I said.

"This is Michael."

My pencil skidded out of the 5 I was trying to complete. I was infuriated by the little jump my heart made, catching my reply in my throat.

"Yes," I said again, my voice clearly disconcerted.

"I'm in town for the day," he said smoothly. "I thought we might have dinner together."

"I think that could be arranged," I said.

He laughed. "Do you? I'll pick you up from work, then."

"I'll want to go home and change," I said.

"Then I'll take you home and wait while you change.

I have to be back fairly early. I want to leave town by eight."

"All right," I said. "Pick me up here." I gave him the address. "I'll be waiting by the front door."

"Good," he said. "I look forward to it."

We hung up. My hands were trembling and I felt my forehead go cool and damp. It occurred to me that I was becoming like someone who thinks every atom that moves in the universe moves with intention toward himself, a kind of thinking I have always detested, perhaps because it would have been so easy for me to espouse. I told myself that Michael's call, coming as it did just when I had given up expecting it (and so, unconsciously expected it the more), was possibly a gratuitous event. At the same time I thought of my desperation the night before, of the letter I had written to him without even knowing how overwhelmingly he was on my mind. I knew that had he called the day before or the day after, he would have talked to a different woman, perhaps a stronger, more sensible one. Now there was nothing to do but see him and spend the rest of the day screwing up my courage to keep quiet about what it meant to me to see him at all.

At four-thirty I was standing expectantly at the curb when a red Volkswagen pulled up and Michael leaned across the seat to open the door on my side. "Get in," he said.

I had a moment's indecision, then climbed in beside him.

He drove off immediately, without looking at me. "Where do you live?" he asked.

"Uptown. Take a right on St. Charles."

He nodded.

"Did you have a good drive down?"

He opened his window, leaned out, watching the cars behind changing lanes. Then he gave me a serious look. "A good drive?"

"I mean, was there a lot of traffic?"

"No."

"I like that drive. I like where the highway goes through the swamps."

"What is it that you like about it?"

"It's so straight. The water is strange, so still."

"That's true."

"I had a client who worked on that highway. He had to stand in chest-deep water, cutting trees with a chain saw. He had to hold the saw up over his head most of the time. He did it for six months. Then he got pneumonia, from the water all the time. Now he can't work any more."

"How did he feel about it?"

"About what?"

"About what happened to him."

"I don't know."

He turned onto St. Charles. "You go all the way to Carrollton," I said.

"You like your job?" he asked.

"I don't mind it."

We were quiet for a few minutes. I looked around the car. It was clean, it smelled new. "Why did you get a red car?" I asked.

"What do you mean?"

"Why red? I didn't think you'd have a red car."

"What did you think I'd have?"

"I imagined it would be gray. Or white. I just didn't think it would be red."

"You tried to imagine what kind of car I would have?"

"I was waiting for you. I wanted to see if I had any idea what I was waiting for."

"And you didn't?"

"No."

"Why should you?"

I opened my purse and took out my cigarettes. "You want one?"

"No."

I lit my cigarette and looked out the window. The ride wasn't unpleasant, but I didn't look forward to arriving at my apartment, going inside. What would I say? I was tired, I didn't know this man at all.

"You're a strange woman," he said, interrupting my fears.

"What's strange about me?"

"How old are you?"

"Twenty-seven."

"Do you want to get married? Have children?"

"With you?"

"No." He smiled with self-satisfaction. "I'm marrying Clarissa."

"We should talk about that," I said.

"I don't see why. It's settled." He pursued his point. "Do you consider yourself a liberated woman?"

"Liberated from what?"

"From men. From needing men?"

"I don't think about it that much."

"Well, think about it."

"I like being grown up," I said. "I like being able to earn a living for myself and having a place of my own."

"That's not what I mean."

"I know," I said. "But I can't answer what you mean."

"Why not?"

"Because . . . when that kind of woman starts to exist, when she is truly that kind of woman, she wouldn't know it, would she? She wouldn't be able to know it."

"Know what?"

"That what was wrong with her was that she didn't need men."

"That would be what was right with her."

"But she wouldn't know. Whether it was right or wrong. If I believed myself to be that kind of woman, my believing it would prove I wasn't. I wouldn't know because it wouldn't be there."

He scowled impatiently. "What wouldn't be there?"

"The need."

"Do you have that, the need? Or don't you? That's all I asked."

"I don't know."

We turned onto Carrollton. "How far?" he asked.

"Three blocks. Then take a right. My house is the third one on the left."

He didn't speak until we pulled up in front of my house. "I don't believe you don't know," he said; then opened his door and got out before I could answer. He walked around the car to open my door.

"I don't care," I said, when I was certain that he wouldn't hear me.

We went inside. Michael followed me through the house to the sun porch. "Would you like some coffee?" I asked.

He bent down to look into the pigeon cage. "Yes," he said. "Are these pets?"

"They're homing pigeons." I put the kettle on the stove and prepared the coffee pot, talking to him from the kitchen.

"Do they come in through this window?"

"I bring them in sometimes, to look at them. I don't like them to stay inside because they sit on my plants and break the leaves."

"Do they have names?"

"The gray one is Gray Bird and the brown one is Brown Bird."

"How original."

When I brought the coffee in, he was picking through a bowl of rocks he'd found on the table. "It's pleasant here," he said. "Have you lived here long?"

"About two years."

"You live alone here."

"Yes."

"Have you ever lived with a man?"

"No, not really. Not for any length of time."

He smiled to himself, as if this was the answer he expected. I was uncomfortable. I wanted to take a shower, eat dinner, and go to sleep. I could think of no way to tell him how tired I was. The letter I had written to him the night before was mixed in with a stack of papers near his elbow. "I wrote you a letter," I said.

"Did you mail it?"

"No."

"Do you want me to read it?"

"I don't know. Maybe later. Not now."

He sipped at his coffee. "The reason I got a red car," he explained, "was because I bought it from a friend of mine and got it cheap. I didn't choose red. I don't like red."

"Oh," I said.

"Oh," he imitated me.

"I want to take a shower and change," I said. "I'm too tired to think."

"Go ahead. I'll wait."

I gathered together a clean dress and some towels and locked myself in the bathroom. I showered quickly but thoroughly and tied my wet hair up in a towel. When I came out Michael had moved to the front room, where I found him going through my records. He had put on a Beethoven quartet.

He didn't look at me as I came in. I thought, watching his hands moving curiously over the records, that I must find some way to make him want me. The idea made me smile. What did I mean by it? I wanted him to want me as badly as I wanted him, to sit at a table far away from me and feel my presence so intolerably that he must take up a pen and write to me, plead with me. As I had written to him. I couldn't tell why I ached so for a man I knew so little about. And what little I did know wasn't admirable.

With feelings like these, I thought, we could never be friends. And yet we must be, in some way, we would have to be. If not, we could only shame each other; we would end trying to find ways to avoid looking at each other.

He turned to me just as this last idea occurred. He smiled as if genuinely pleased to see me, as if it were a surprise to be pleased. "Do you feel better?" he asked.

"Yes." I sat down on the couch. He stood in front of me, unbuttoning the sleeves of my dress.

"I like these dresses you wear," he said. "They're flowing, sort of breezy."

"They come off easy," I said.

He slipped his hand under my skirt and ran his forefinger along the lace at the edge of my pants, then, as I lifted my hips, pulled them off in a single movement. I sat forward a little to help him as he pulled my dress over my head.

"Are you shy of me?" he asked.

"A little."

"Do you mind?"

"No. I like it." I unbuttoned his shirt and he quickly removed his other clothes. I believe both of us intended to go into the bedroom, but once we started, we couldn't stop. He was powerful and terrifying, as he had not been before. I felt myself opening, at first against my will, and then with my consent, opening and opening to him so that behind my eyelids I saw hundreds of doors flying open, one after another, and I knew these were the doors behind which I usually hid, through which no one passed, not even myself. I experienced the sensation of being flooded by a kind of light, like water, and being open to this flood, although it was blinding, because it was blinding. I felt that he felt this too, that he knew he could go on and on with this and I would still be opening to him, that this was not an ordinary coupling where bodies rise and fall together, at best a balanced contest of giving and taking. This was all his giving and all my being taken, taking, opening like a series of doors falling one into another, a stack of cards opening in a spiral, or being sucked through whirlpool after whirlpool, and always falling into another and going deeper and deeper. I experienced the sensation of falling, even as I had a mental picture of hitting ground. Like falling out of a tree, there is a split second when the body surrend-

126

ers to the fall, to the sensation of the fall—I'm falling—even as every atom of the mind concentrates on the impact to come, on preparing for that impact, with every muscle of the body which is, after that second is over, that long second, at its disposal—I'm hitting ground. I fell through that moment again and again, falling, hitting ground that gave way beneath me, and falling again. Michael fell with me and through me. I was always there to meet him, I was the ground beneath him, meeting him and giving way to him. He went through me and past me, but whenever it seemed that he might have gone beyond me, there I was again, meeting him, giving way beneath him.

On a couch. When we were done he still had his socks on. It occurred to me that anyone watching us would have laughed, and I laughed with exhaustion. I could not think what had happened. Another ten minutes lost, I thought, was it ten? I would never be able to account for them. I had felt myself opening like a time-lapse film of a flower, a knot of gray that opens red and startling yellow.

"We picked up where we left off," he said, looking so contented that I felt, for the first time, secure in my own perception of what was going on between us. We talked for a few moments. He asked me questions with obvious answers and I was too stunned then to consider what I said. He rubbed his palm against my cheek and sat up abruptly. "That was very nice," he said. He went to change the record. I sat up too, dazed and disheveled, defenseless. He pulled his pants on and sat on the floor to put on his shoes, his back to me. I made no movement. He turned to me. "What are you doing?" he said.

"I can't move."

He looked annoyed. "Get dressed," he said. "We'll go out to eat."

"Give me a minute."

"All right," he said. He walked out of the room. I heard the bathroom door close.

I reached for my dress and pulled it over my head, but didn't have the energy to push my arms through the sleeves. This is bad, I thought over and over. I need to lie down. I stretched out on my side, my dress gathered up around my neck. I heard Michael walking in the next room. Then I felt he was standing in the doorway looking at me. I didn't care to look at him. He said nothing. After a few moments I sat up and pulled on my dress. I picked up my pants and went past him to the bathroom, where I washed my face and crotch quickly with a cool washcloth. I looked at my blank expression in the mirror. This is how I'll look when I'm dead, I thought. Then I finished dressing and joined Michael in the living room. I sat next to him. "Why are you marrying Clarissa?" I asked.

"Because I want to."

"Why did you come here?"

"I think you know."

"No. I don't. Tell me."

"It's hard to explain," he said. "You could call it a compulsion." He laughed joylessly. "A man's got to do what he's got to do."

"Is that your philosophy?"

"Sure," he said. "What do you think of it?"

I got up and walked to the bedroom door. "I think it sucks," I said.

He laughed again. "I'm used to the idea that good things don't last."

128

I sneered. "No, they won't, if you think like that."

"They won't," he said seriously, "no matter what you think."

I considered this. Did I believe it? No, I thought obstinately, I don't believe that. I went into the back room and cleared up the coffee cups. Michael followed me aimlessly. "Where do you want to eat?"

"I don't care."

"Is there some place near here?"

"Yes," I said. "A few blocks away. We can walk there."

"I'd like to spend more time," he said, "but I have to be back early."

"I understand," I said.

"Do you?"

"You want to get away from me."

"Why do you say that? Do you want me to deny it?"

"Let's go," I said.

The restaurant was quiet and we ate quickly, not talking much. Michael warmed a little to me, I imagined, because he could see how weary I was, how unlikely I was to demand anything. We walked back to my apartment and stood on the steps talking.

"I don't know when I'll be in town again," he said. "Probably in a few weeks. Before the wedding, anyway."

"When is the wedding?"

"Three weeks. You'll be there, of course."

I tore off one of my fingernails with my teeth. "I don't think I would enjoy it," I said.

"Clarissa would be hurt if you stayed away."

"I suppose so," I said. "I guess I'll have to come."

"But I'll see you again before that."

"If you like," I said.

He took my hand, found it limp, and released me. "I'll call," he said.

I stood on the steps until he had driven away. Then I went inside, closing and locking the door behind me.

❀ 7

It was the next night that I began to have difficulty sleeping. I came home from work, bathed, and cooked a simple meal, passing the evening reading a book which failed to interest me. Reed called just as I was preparing for bed and we agreed to meet the following evening.

"That guy Richard was in the bar last night," he said.

"You didn't say anything to him."

"I couldn't. He was too drunk. I think he's having a breakdown or something. He looks weird."

"Weird?"

"He talks to himself and he's always slapping at his face like there's bugs around. He's a fruitcake."

"I know," I said.

"Does his wife know?"

"I think she does."

"Keep away from him."

"I will," I promised.

We hung up. I turned off the light and lay in bed looking around the room. I had the illusion that the bedroom door was being pushed open, then pulled shut again. I turned away and looked at the wall. I searched for a fantasy that would help me to sleep. Foolishly, embarrassed to feel the comfort I took in it, I imagined a telephone conversation with Michael in which he told me he couldn't marry Clarissa. "Because of you," he said. I went over that phrase again and again and began to doze. As I was slipping from light to deep sleep, I awoke with a start. The door had flown open and slammed against the wall. Someone was standing over me.

I sat up and looked around the quiet room. The door was half closed. I fell back on my pillow. I was sweating and I felt stifled.

I got up and walked around the house. It was too late to play a record, it would wake the people downstairs. I made some hot milk, standing naked at the stove and drinking it in a few gulps.

I went back to bed. Each time I began to sleep I woke up suddenly, thinking I had heard a noise or sensed a presence near me.

As soon as sunlight began to filter through the thin curtains, I got up and put on a robe. I sat in the back room watching my pigeons until it was time to dress and go to work.

In the week that followed, this became a pattern. Unable to sleep at night, I dozed at my desk in the afternoon. I had more and more difficulty keeping up with my work. My interviews were uneventful and painstakingly thorough. I couldn't trust myself to remember what my clients told me and so I wrote everything down.

Maggie and I gave up trying to have lunch together. It seemed one or the other of us always had too much work or an appointment scheduled. I told her about Michael's visit briefly over coffee. She pretended interest, but I had the feeling she was thinking of something else. I thought I knew what. I questioned her about Richard a few times but she closed the subject quickly. He was all right. He was painting a lot and the long baths had stopped.

I saw Reed every few days. He noticed my insomnia the first night we spent together, though he didn't say anything about it until morning. It was a Sunday, and as I had passed the night tossing beside him, when I fell asleep toward daybreak he didn't try to rouse me. I slept until noon. When I woke he was sitting in a chair drawn up to the bed, looking at me.

I smiled. "What time is it?"

"You were dreaming," he said.

"I don't remember."

"Your eyes were moving."

"How long have you been sitting there?"

"How come you couldn't sleep last night?"

"I don't know. Lately that happens a lot."

"I could get you some pills."

"I guess I'll try that soon. I get so tired, I think I've got to sleep, but when I lie down, I can't."

"Are you hungry?"

I stretched. "Yes. I feel a little better. I haven't slept that much in days."

Reed got up and I followed him to the kitchen. He opened the refrigerator and stood gazing inside. "Nothing in here but eggs."

"No bread?"

He opened a cabinet. "I've got bread." He put the bread on the table. "I'll go get some milk."

After we had eaten, Reed cleared off the table and

prepared to take some Nembutal. He talked as he was emptying the capsules into the spoon. "You can sleep the rest of the day here," he said.

"I feel like I could. If you don't mind."

"No. I like to have you here. The reason you can sleep here is because you know you're safe here."

"I guess so."

He laughed. "My bed's not too good."

"It's O.K."

"I need to put a board in it."

The drug was ready and I watched him jam the needle into his vein. He wiped the blood away with the flat of his hand so that it smeared on his arm, then dropped the syringe into a glass of water. "You're so rough with yourself," I said. I dipped a napkin into the water and took his hand so I could wash the ugly red mark off his arm.

"It doesn't matter." He pulled me onto his lap for a long embrace. Then I rested my head against his shoulder and he stroked my hair gently. We sat like that for some time.

"Are you asleep?" he asked.

"Almost."

"I'll put you to bed."

We roused ourselves and went into the bedroom. I was asleep almost as soon as my head touched the pillow. When I woke up, hours later, Reed was sitting by the bed, drowsily guarding my sleep.

"Is it late?" I asked.

"No. I don't know." There was a loud knocking at the front door. "Oh, shit," Reed said. "Who could that be?"

I sat up and looked around for my clothes.

"Don't worry," Reed said, going to the door. "Whoever it is isn't staying."

I fell back and listened to the sound of voices at the door, Reed's and a woman's. After a few minutes Reed came back in, closing the door behind him.

"Who is it?" I asked.

"Oh, this dumb girl. Her old man threw her out so she came here."

"She's still here?"

"She's in the kitchen. She's hungry. She was on the street all night."

"I'd better go," I said.

"I told her you were here. She just wants to get off the street."

"Still," I said, pulling on my blouse, "I should be going. I've got some stuff to do at home."

Reed sat on the bed and watched me dress. "If you can't sleep," he said, "come back here. You want my car?"

"No. I'll be all right."

He followed me through the house. As I passed the kitchen I saw a young woman sitting at the table buttering slices of bread and drinking milk. "Hi," I said. She smiled at me vaguely, pushing her long hair out of her face. At the door Reed kissed me. He nodded over his shoulder toward the kitchen. "I'm sorry about this."

"Don't be silly," I said. "I'll call you later."

He closed the door behind me and I found myself standing dazed in the dull light of the street. The sun was going down. I had slept all day. How would I spend the evening? I walked through the Quarter toward Canal. I was thinking about Michael.

What was he doing? Where was he? Was he thinking of me? I was going over something he had said, over and over it. It was after we had made love. We lay face to face, our legs intertwined. He kissed my hairline and rubbed his hand against my jaw, a habit he had, as if he wanted to break my face, feeling for the places where it would most easily come apart. He said, looking at me, making me meet his eyes, "Do you like to feel me inside you?" The question embarrassed me but I said "Yes," and clearly enough before I looked away. Now I thought over that question. Why had he asked me that? Surely my behavior made the answer obvious. He hadn't asked it to find out anything. What had he wanted, to say such a thing? He wanted to hear me say, "Yes, I do want you." It was important that I said it, heard myself say it. Was that it? I went over it a few more times, his question, my answer. The truth became clear to me against my own will, like watching blood gather to the edges of a razor wound. It wasn't a flash of understanding. He wanted to humiliate me. He wanted me to say, "Yes, I want to be screwed by you, I need it. I need to be humiliated by you." My obtuseness in not having seen this before made me nauseous. At the same time I was pleased, and it amused me more than a little. Humiliate me? I thought. Poor bastard. I couldn't imagine what pleasure he would get from that. He might as well try to humiliate a worm. How disappointed he must have been to see how little it mattered to me, what I said, what he did to me. It was possible that he didn't even know what he was doing. Or why he was doing it. And here I was, accidentally holding the upper hand. I thought I might call Clarissa. "Look, don't marry that guy. Take my word for it, I can't tell you how I know, but don't do it."

But I couldn't tell her. It occurred to me that he might not have the same intentions toward Clarissa as he had toward me. Or he might already have accomplished his purpose. I imagined Clarissa confessing to all sorts of inclinations, toward perversions she had never even thought about. She would lose her self-respect, but worse things could happen than that. Self-respect was a word I had heard Michael use on two or three occasions. It seemed to have some meaning for him. Or was he merely testing it on me? He had asked me about other men and I had told him about Reed. And could I keep my self-respect with Reed? he wanted to know. With him? He had asked that, when we had dinner together, and the answer seemed important to him. I couldn't remember what I had said. I thought I had said, "Yes, I could." Obviously a challenge. No wonder he came back for more. What would he do when he realized—he would have to sooner or later—that the word meant nothing to me, that the loss of that commodity was as insignificant to me as paring a fingernail?

A week passed. I received an invitation to Clarissa's wedding. It was to take place in the evening of the following Friday. I knew as I stood looking at the small, precisely printed card that no matter whose feelings were hurt I wouldn't be able to go. I resolved to send a telegram saying I was ill, sending congratulations and regrets. Would I see Michael again before this? I believed I would.

But I didn't. The day of the wedding arrived and I spent the morning dazedly interviewing clients. In the afternoon I painstakingly composed my telegram and phoned it into the telegraph office. I imagined Clarissa's preparations, the last-minute instructions to her children, the short drive to the small and tasteful chapel where she would seal what I could only regard as a questionable bargain. I picked up the phone a few times, preparing to call her, to warn her, but each time I put it down with the conviction that the solution to the problem could best be found in my silence. I didn't know Michael well enough, nor did I know how well Clarissa knew him. I might only confuse them both by unburdening myself of a guilt that had nothing to do with the terms of their alliance. I spent the next week in sleepless and dreamy suspense. On Saturday morning, as I was going out to Reed's, where I hoped to spend the rest of the day asleep, I was jarred from all sensibility by the sight of a red Volkswagen pulling up to my curb. Clarissa stepped out on the passenger side and Michael, who was driving, pulled away from the curb without looking at me. I stood on the steps looking shamefacedly at Clarissa. Her expression confirmed a suspicion I had not even had the courage to formulate consciously. She had come to tell me what she knew.

I went down a few steps to meet her. "It's good to see you," I said uselessly.

"I've got to talk to you," she said. "I was going to call, but I decided that it would be better to see you. So I could be sure."

We had reached the landing and she followed me inside.

"Be sure of what?" I asked. "Do you want some coffee, or iced tea?"

She appraised me thoughtfully. "If you don't know, I'm in more trouble than I thought," she said.

"I know," I said, looking down. "At least I think I know."

"I won't play a guessing game," she said. "He tells me he's been having an affair with you."

"I don't know if I would describe it that way," I said.

"Well, how would you describe it?"

"Look," I said, "can't we sit down? I'm not sure I know what you've come for."

She preceded me to the back room. "Jesus, it's hot," she said. "It's worse here than in Baton Rouge."

"You want some tea?" I asked again.

"Yes," she said. "No sugar."

I was eager for a chance not to be observed. I poured two glasses of tea and filled them with ice. My hands were shaking badly. If only I'd slept, I thought. I brought the glasses in and sat down across from Clarissa. She picked up her glass and pressed it against her forehead. "I'm really upset," she said. "I don't think I know why I came, either. He told me this yesterday, right out of the blue. I thought I had to confront you to make sure it was true. Now I don't know what I've got on my hands." She wiped her forehead with the back of her hand and looked at me curiously. "Why didn't you tell me? Is that why you didn't come to the wedding?"

"I wanted to tell you," I said. "I almost did, that day I came up and you said you were going to marry him. I started to tell you. But I couldn't. I thought—I don't know —I thought maybe you knew."

"I knew?" she sputtered. "This is terrible."

"You must hate me," I said. "I don't have any idea what to say."

"I don't know how I feel," she said. "How long has this been going on?"

"Since that time I came to see you and you were at your mother's. I didn't know who he was. I went out to

139

L.S.U. looking for you and I found him. I didn't know you were going to marry him."

"He said you knew."

"I didn't. How could I?"

"No. I know I hadn't told you then."

"I'm relieved that you know."

"*I'm* not. Why did he tell me? I can't figure it out."

"What did he say?"

"I said I was going to ask you up next weekend and he said no, he didn't think I really wanted to do that, and then he told me, well . . . I hate to say it."

"What?"

"He said you were in love with him and that if *I* didn't catch on, he was sure the children would. And then he said, anyway, you were such a slut he didn't see what I saw in you."

I concentrated on my tea. "What did you say?"

"Well, the idea of you being in love with anybody didn't strike me as very plausible," she said, laughing. "I mean, I know you better than I know him. At least I thought I did. *Are* you in love with him?"

I smiled. "Not any more."

"You're not going on with this thing, then? I mean, if you are, I want to know."

"No. I don't want to see somebody who calls me a slut."

She gave me an incredulous look. "Where is he coming from with that? I couldn't believe it. Did he think I was going to say, 'Gee, thanks for telling me'? He's not what I thought, and this proves it."

"You're being kind," I said. "I feel guilty as hell. I don't know how you can forgive me so easily."

"Why should you feel guilty?" she observed. "Whatever else he is, he's an unusual man, and it doesn't surprise me that you would be curious. I'm not hurt or anything. It's not as if I didn't understand what you did."

"But what?"

"But why did he tell me? It's so stupid. What did he hope to accomplish?"

"To come between us?"

"At least that."

"He's cruel," I said. "It's as if he were driven to it and he couldn't help himself. I've met men like him before. And honesty is always a weapon for them. They use it to whip their victims into submission. And then they deny it. They don't see it when everyone else does. Do you know what I mean?"

"That he's compulsive?"

"Well, yes. I guess I'm just trying to say I don't think he's consciously cruel. If he were, he'd be more subtle. At least, I hope he's not."

"Because if he is, he's a fool."

"One would rather believe anything than that."

Clarissa laughed. "He thinks I came in here to threaten your life or something. To say, 'Keep away from my man.'"

"Then you were angry?"

"I was. But that seems like so much foolishness. I was just stunned."

"I'm sorry."

She shrugged. "Maybe it's better. Now you know what I couldn't tell you before. Though I wanted to."

"What?"

She paused, expecting me to guess. "Why I married him. I mean, he's made love to you. So you know."

"Oh, Clarissa," I said. My eyes filled with tears and I held a burst of laughter in my throat. "Yes, I do know."

141

She covered her face with her hand. "Isn't this hell?" She sighed.

"I won't see him again," I said.

"No," she agreed. "Don't. Try not to."

"What will you do?"

"I don't know. I'll have to think about it."

"It may be something that won't happen again."

"That's not likely," she said. She finished her tea and smiled. "I guess I'll go. I told him I'd meet him at Compania's."

"I won't see you for a while."

"No," she said. "I think not."

We walked to the door and stood on the step talking for a few minutes before she left. We were both surprised and ill at ease at how easily we had settled this matter between us, how clearly we saw one another's position. When she had gone I wondered what she would say to him about our talk. I suspected she would say as little as possible. I assumed that Michael wouldn't try to see me again.

I went to Reed's, and before I feel asleep I told him of Clarissa's visit.

"Then forget it," he said impatiently. "It's over. It was a mistake."

"I know," I said. "It just floors me to be so completely wrong."

"About him?"

"Sure."

"But you always knew about him."

"I guess so," I said. "I guess I did."

Reed looked at the clock. "Are you in a hurry?" I asked. "Am I in the way?"

"I've got to pick up some stuff in half an hour. Can you sleep without me here?"

"Just stay a few minutes," I said. "I'm so tired."

He sat on the edge of the bed waiting for me to sleep. As I was drifting into a thick, viscous blackness that seemed always to be lurking at the edge of my consciousness, I felt him get up and leave the room. "What kind of stuff?" I mumbled, but he didn't hear me.

He didn't come back that day. I woke up after eight, soaking in sweat. The room was dark and the air was so heavy and damp it clung to me like a blanket. I remembered a story Reed had told me, of a man who searched for a basic thought pattern. He took a large dose of LSD, immersed himself to the neck in water the temperature of his blood, and floated there in absolute darkness. After a while, Reed said, he gave up listening to his thoughts and concluded that there were no basic patterns, no symbols, just an infinite regression, a continual falling. The story had astounded me, not because of what the man found, but because I couldn't imagine anyone having the courage to take such a chance with his own sanity. I listened to my thoughts. The usual jumble, and through it all a kind of buzzing, like wires burning out. Did some minds work better than others, like watches? Did some people think clearly, know what they were thinking all the time? My head ached. "I'll swim out of this bed," I said into the empty, clammy air. Then I got up, dressed, and went home. Later that night I called Reed at the bar. "You got the stuff all right?" I asked. I knew the answer, his speech was slurred with it.

"I almost had to kill the guy to get it," he said. "But it was worth it."

"What is it?"

"The real thing. Don't guess on the phone."

"All right, then," I said. "I'll call you tomorrow."

But I didn't call. The next morning, as I was cursing over a pot of boiling coffee, the phone rang. I won't answer it, I thought, but did so involuntarily and nearly slammed the receiver back down when I recognized the voice that said my name. "What do you want?" I asked.

"I'm in town," Michael replied. "I have a few hours."

"Are you kidding?"

He was amused. "I don't think I am."

"No," I complained. "No. I don't want to see you. Not after all that shit yesterday. Why would I want to see you?"

"Are you angry because I told Clarissa?"

"Michael," I said, "why did you do that?"

"I thought she should know. I don't see how it changes anything."

For one vicious moment I didn't see how it changed anything either. Then, because I couldn't trust myself to say anything adequate, I set the receiver carefully into its cradle.

I returned to my coffee. My hands were shaking. I didn't know what I would do if the phone rang again. I was still considering my options when the doorbell rang.

I opened the door and scowled at Michael, who was leaning against the porch railing. "Go away," I said.

He smiled. "I'm glad to see you again." He passed me and went inside.

I followed, but refused to sit down. I went to the doorway and looked at him coldly. "How was the wedding?"

"It was quiet. Uneventful."

"I didn't get to ask Clarissa about it."

"No? Well, too bad you weren't able to come."

"I was able."

He pressed his palm into the cushion next to him. "Why don't you come and sit here. Have you had any breakfast?"

"Why did you tell her?" I said.

"I told you. I thought she should know."

"What made you think that?"

"Do you usually keep such secrets from your friends?"

"I don't usually *have* such secrets."

"Well, haven't you two talked it over, made it up? What difference does it make?"

"The only reason I can think of that you would do something so . . . foolish is that you meant to be cruel. To her and to me."

"I haven't come here to be cruel."

"I don't know why you came here. I don't care. I want you to go away."

"You know why I'm here as well as I do. Why pretend outraged decency?"

I sighed. "I don't know you," I said. "I don't know what you're like. I won't presume that you think like I think. I'd appreciate it if you'd show me the same courtesy."

"We're strangers." He shrugged. "I don't mind."

"You've hurt Clarissa needlessly, and you've hurt me. Are we nothing?"

"*You've* done that. You would have been more hurt if I hadn't come. If I never called again. Then you would count yourself abused. Please stop this."

I turned away and went into the kitchen. He didn't

145

follow. I stood looking at the dishes in the sink. I heard him put on a record. The feebleness of my resistance shamed me. I opened the back door and looked down the stairs. I felt in my pocket and found some change, enough to get a streetcar downtown. Should I leave a note? The thought made me smile. I hurried down the stairs and across the back yard. How long would he wait there? I felt wildly free and cheerful. I wished I'd brought my checkbook so that I might shop downtown. But it's Sunday, I thought. I hurried along, delighted with my escape. I didn't know where I was going.

When I got to Canal Street I called Reed, but he didn't answer. I walked aimlessly down Royal, looking in the shop windows, staying in the shade of the buildings as much as possible. On the corner of St. Peter an old black man sat on a bench in the full sun playing "Just a Closer Walk with Thee" on a trumpet. His hat lay on the ground at his feet, though it would have done him more good on his head. The sun was so bright on his face that he had closed his eyes resolutely against it. Perspiration streamed over his forehead and down his back. I leaned against a wall for a few minutes listening to his solemn, eerily calm music. It's a funeral song, I thought, and moved on.

Still in good spirits, I wandered across Jackson Square and into the Pontalba museum. I thought I would try to find out why Madame Pontalba's father-in-law had shot her. I asked an old man who looked after the family's relics and he was eager to tell me all he knew. He had never heard that she was shot in the hands. "It was in the hip," he insisted. "He wanted her to sign her money over to him and she wouldn't. She was strong-willed. She did as she pleased."

And got shot for it, I thought. The man amused me, following me around from display to display and talking of the family as if they had only recently moved away. "Are you from here?" he asked as I was leaving.

"Yes," I said. "I've always lived here."

"I knew it," he said.

"How did you know?"

He cocked his head to one side as if to ask himself the question. "You're not in a hurry," he said. "Come back again. I'm always here."

I promised that I would. I spent the next few hours wandering around the streets, eating ice cream on the steps of the cathedral, talking to the portrait painters on the Square. By the afternoon I was exhausted and took a bus to Canal, then a streetcar home.

Michael was gone. I looked around for a note or some sign that he had been there. Nothing. I wondered how long he had stayed. I kicked off my sandals and collapsed in my bed, drifting to sleep without taking off my dress. I was certain, this time, that I wouldn't see him again. His pride would never allow him to seek me out, and I thought, with a sense of failure, I would not be fool enough to try to see him.

8

I was late for work the next morning and I had barely time to straighten my desk and look through my cases when my first appointment, Miss Cunningham, arrived. Maggie wasn't in yet and I assumed that she had taken a much needed day off. I resolved to call her and try to arrange a luncheon date. We had been, of late, out of touch with each other. I was thinking of her when I called out Miss Cunningham's name in the waiting room, and I paid little attention to the young pregnant black woman who stood up and followed me to the interviewing booth.

"My name is Helene Thatcher," I said as we sat down facing each other across the table. I opened her case record and glanced at the three pages inside. Apparently Miss Cunningham had never applied for food stamps before. I disliked such cases; it meant a lot of explaining. The first thing was to dispense with the new client's invariable and insupportable notion that she could talk casually about her situation and I would miraculously solve her problems. "Have you ever had food stamps before?" I asked, looking at Miss Cunningham's face for the first time.

Her expression was blank. She crossed her arms loosely over her unborn child. "I had 'em in Laplace."

I looked at her quizzically. There was something familiar about her voice, the flatness of it. Her eyes met mine, steadily, coolly. She was waiting for me to think up my next question.

"Was that last month?" I asked.

"A few months ago."

"Do you live by yourself?"

"I live in my brother's house. But he don't eat with me."

"Does he buy your food?"

"Not now. I had some money with me when I came here. I buy my own food and I eat by myself. I don't keep my food with his. I keeps mine in a box."

"Do you want to continue this arrangement?"

"I want to get out of his house." She tapped her swollen stomach. "But how can I with this comin'?"

It was hot in the narrow room and I felt unaccountably embarrassed to be asking this woman these foolish questions. At the same time I was secure in my knowledge that, no matter how I felt, the questions would come out in the right order, and that if she tried to hedge on the answers, or if she became hostile, or if she proved incapable of remembering what had happened last month or last week, I would be able to handle it. I felt as a prostitute must feel who discovers that she despises a regular and financially generous client—I could close my mind, turn off every spontaneous response, and do it. My questions materialized, one after the other. I jotted

150

down her answers. She took no interest in the interview, answering me as simply as possible.

"When is your baby due?"

"In November."

"You have no other children?"

"No," she said seriously. "This be my first."

"Are you married or have you ever been married?" I looked away; some clients were embarrassed by this question. Her no was as uninterested as all her other answers.

As we approached the last few questions, I realized that she was eligible and that I would certify her case and never see her again. But where had I seen her before? Her voice, her dull expression, even her manner, the way she pulled unconsciously at her clothes and seemed always on the verge of drifting away from me, all seemed, not just familiar, but somehow dear to me. "Are you sure you've never applied here before?" I asked.

She gave me a condescending frown. "I never been here before. I never been in this building."

I looked at her application. As she spoke I recalled where I had seen her before. On the highway, going to Baton Rouge. That first time I saw Michael. I was sure she knew it, remembered me. She had lost me that night and would lose me again, nor did it seem strange to her, I thought, that I should twice stand between her and what she wanted.

"Is that all?" she asked. "Can I go now?"

I looked at her curiously. Perhaps she didn't know me. Was she the same woman? I couldn't tell.

"Yes," I said. "I'll show you how to get to the stairs."

She followed me docilely, and I stood at the top of the stairs watching her back recoil from the strain of each step as she went down. Her name was Ella, I thought. I flipped through the application and checked the name. It was Mae Ella Cunningham. It *was* her; I was convinced. I wanted to know what had happened to her that night. I had a fantasy, as I hurried down the stairs, that I would tell her about Michael, about what that night had come to mean to me. I rushed past a man who was struggling to get a suitcase through the downstairs door and out into the street. "Ella," I called. I saw her turning the corner. I ran after her, called her name again, brushing carelessly against a man who yelled after me, "Watch where you're going." The morning sun struck me full in the face as I rounded the corner and said her name softly, once more, to the dazzling and empty street.

She had escaped me twice, I thought, we were strangers. I wondered confusedly what I had hoped to say to her, to get from her. I turned abruptly and made my way back to the office, unable to quell an insidious suspicion that she knew something about me no one else knew. How useless I was. To myself. I couldn't listen to these thoughts.

I went back to my desk and hastily did the computations on her case. I wanted to be done with it. My phone rang and Maggie's supervisor asked me to come to her office, then changed her mind and said she would come to my desk.

"Have you heard from Maggie this morning?" she asked when she arrived.

"No. Didn't she call?"

She seated herself casually at Maggie's desk. "No, she didn't. That's not like her. I thought maybe you knew where she was."

"I'll call her house," I said, picking up the phone. I dialed Maggie's number and listened to a tape recording which informed me that the line was disconnected. I dialed again, listened to the first few words of the tape, and hung up. Maggie's supervisor flipped through the cases on her desk.

"She's got six people to see today. I'll have to reassign them."

"The line's disconnected," I said.

She sorted a stack of cases and stood up. "I hope nothing's wrong. If you hear from her, call me."

"I will," I said. I had a sudden picture of Richard pulling the phone cord out of the wall.

When had I last seen Maggie, what had she said? I couldn't remember. I was irritable the rest of the day. I wanted to go to her apartment at lunch but two clients came in unexpectedly and I had to eat a sandwich quickly at my desk. I decided to leave work at three, I would say I was ill. At two-thirty I finished my last interview and arrived at my desk just in time to answer the phone.

"Helene?" Maggie said.

"At last. Are you O.K.? Where are you?"

"I'm at DePaul's hospital."

"What happened?"

"Richard." She paused, sounding too tired to go on. "He had a breakdown. He burned the apartment."

"He burned your apartment?"

"I can't talk about it now."

"What can I do?"

"Tell my supervisor there was a fire. Tell her I won't be in tomorrow either."

"Sure. Where are you going?"

She paused again, then said, as if the answer pleased her, "I don't know."

"Stay at my house tonight. You can take a bus over now. There's a key in the shed, in the back, just inside the door. It's on a can of turpentine."

"I don't know," she said again.

"Please, Maggie, you've got to stay somewhere. You should go there now and rest."

"Yes," she agreed. "I'd like a bath. I'm so tired."

"When did this happen?"

"It started this morning, about five. It took a long time. I was at Charity for hours trying to get him out of there."

"He's all right?" I asked. "He wasn't hurt?"

"No. He wasn't hurt."

"You'll go to my house, then," I said.

"Yes. I'll go there now. I'll see you when you get home."

"Good," I said. "Rest. You should rest now. Do you have tranquillizers?"

She laughed. "That's the one thing every doctor I talked to made sure I had. *I* didn't burn the house, *he* did."

"I'm sorry," I said.

She laughed softly again. "I'm all right," she said. "I'll see you later."

We hung up. I sat back in my chair, too stunned to think of anything in particular, my head buzzing with questions. After a few minutes I went to tell Maggie's supervisor, as briefly as possible, what had happened.

154

When I got home I heard water running in the bathroom. Maggie's purse was on the couch and a dress I didn't recognize hung on the hook outside the bathroom door. I tapped on the door.

"Helene?"

I raised my voice to be heard over the water. "Yes."

"Come in," she said.

I opened the door to find her stretched out in the tub, half covered with water and bubbles. "I used your bath stuff," she said. "I hope you don't mind."

"No. Help yourself."

"I did." She folded a washcloth and placed it over her eyes. "I ate some eggs, too. I was so hungry. I didn't get here until a half hour ago. I spent the whole day arguing with those bastard doctors."

"How do you feel?"

She pushed the cloth away and sat up. "Relieved." She began rubbing soap into the cloth. "I'm glad I came here."

"You can stay here for a while."

"You've really changed it a lot. The sun room is great. I watched your pigeons for a while." She talked nervously, then laughed abruptly. "I don't have a thing. It's all gone."

"How bad is the apartment."

"I didn't really see it. When I left, it was still burning. But I called the girl in the slave quarter and she said the front house is just a shell. All she had was smoke damage. She said by the time the firemen really got going, the top half of the building had caved in. They spent the rest of the time wetting down her place and the buildings on the side to keep it from spreading."

"Is it still burning?"

155

"It's smoldering. That's what she said, anyway. I haven't any insurance. What if the landlord sues me?"

"I don't think he can."

"Everyone knows Richard started it. The whole neighborhood saw him screaming about it."

"Why did he do it?"

"I don't think he knows." She dropped back into the water to rinse off the soap. "I've got to get out of here, I'm melting."

The bathroom was dripping from steam. I got her a clean towel and stood in the open door watching her dry off. She was careless, rubbing the towel against her legs, wrapping it loosely around her waist. She stumbled against the sink, then leaned against it, dropping her head wearily. I gave her a robe. "Do you want some iced tea?" I asked.

"That would be good." Her hand caught in the sleeve; she pushed it through roughly, then rubbed at a mark on her arm.

"They gave you a shot?"

She sat down awkwardly on the john, hiding her face in her hands. When she looked up, her eyes were filled with tears. "I feel so bad," she moaned. The robe had fallen open, revealing her breasts. I had a strong desire to put my arms around her and kiss her, but the thought of the pain this would undoubtedly cause us both made me take a determined step backward. She pulled the robe closed and stood up.

"It's the sedation," I said. "You've been up too long. Why don't you get in bed and I'll bring you some tea. Then you can sleep."

She nodded. I went to the bed and pulled back the

156

sheets, then went to the kitchen to make tea. When I came back she was lying on her back with the sheet pulled up to her nose, her eyes closed. I set her glass on the nightstand, thinking she was asleep. She opened her eyes and looked at me vaguely, then pulled herself up to drink. When she had finished she gave me the glass with a sleepy smile. "It's so nice here," she said.

"Go to sleep," I said. "It won't be hard."

She sighed. "No. I'm tired. I'm dead." She lay back and closed her eyes. For a moment I wanted to shake her awake and ask her hundreds of questions. Then, embarrassed by my impatience, I began to prepare some food for when she woke up.

She slept for eight hours. When the dinner was thoroughly cold I ate some from the dish in which it was cooked. I drank coffee and sat in the back room disconsolately, tired but determined to stay awake.

I thought. First I thought about Maggie, imagining the day she had been through, wondering if I would have handled such a sequence of events as well. Or would I have done better? I thought of Richard and these were guilty thoughts. I was certain I should have told Maggie of his peculiar behavior, should have realized something was going wrong when he stopped following me weeks ago. It surprised me to find that I knew this. He had been following me and then he had stopped. After that night in the cathedral. Should I have spoken to him then? I remembered how much I had enjoyed that night and knew I had not spoken because I was afraid he would ruin it. It was a dream I was having and I would not have it spoiled.

I thought of Michael. Suppose he called me, appeared

at my door. I regretted running from him. I regretted running. Am I changing? I thought. Is something changing me?

I thought of Reed and I recalled how we had met, the understanding of our first meeting. I was dancing in a bar and I was aware of him, on the fringe of the crowd surrounding the dance floor, watching me. My dance partner didn't interest me but I was enjoying my own dancing, the fact of it. Several men had asked me to dance or expressed pleasure in watching me. I did not, ordinarily, care to draw this kind of attention to myself, but on this evening every eye that settled on me seemed to contain some tacit and innocent approval and I enjoyed it. It was not me but the motion I was in that attracted notice, so that everyone who saw me must desire to be in motion as well. As I danced I was aware of Reed standing up; his eyes had rested on me so long I felt the loss when he looked away. I knew he was moving in my direction, past me, toward the door. I had my back to him when he turned and lunged through the crowd of dancers, but when his arms slipped around my shoulders, I knew it was he. He lifted me from the floor effortlessly and carried me through the crowd, which separated mindlessly, to a French door that should have opened into the street. The door was locked and he cursed it vigorously. Over his shoulder I saw the bartender pushing toward us through the crowd, his face angry and intent. Reed kicked at the door. "Try the other door," I suggested, and he turned like an animal who has just heard his own idea, shouldering his way back through the crowd and out into the street. He put me down, pressing me against a wall in a long, sleepily passionate embrace that I returned warmly. When he

158

released me he caressed my neck, saying softly, "What can you do? What can you do?" Later I wondered what he had meant. Did he mean what could one (anyone) do, or what, exactly, could *I* do. But I didn't think of that then. I was filled with a practical desire to get off the street. "Where can we go?" I countered.

"This way," he said, taking my hand and leading me, without speaking again, the four blocks to his apartment.

A peculiar beginning, I thought, but gradually he had come to be what he was to me, a safe harbor. Was it only time that had made him this? Certainly he could be treacherous. But I knew him, I felt I knew where he would fail me, and I him, and these were not intentional failures, not acts of any kind, only the absence of will. I lingered over some recollections of our lovemaking, always the good-natured coupling of sleepy lovers who seek in one another's embrace not stimulation but the egress to unconsciousness, to dark, warm oblivion. Reed's energy amazed me. He could take enough dope to level most people and then find delight in a burst of sexual energy; he used it to push himself over the last painful limits of consciousness. My pleasure was in watching him drift away, fighting it as if he did not wish to go, hanging on to me, fighting again. Sometimes he shook his head so vigorously it seemed he would break his neck, trying to block out the darkness that swept over his limbs and unfocused his eyes, and sighing that he would not leave me yet, no not just yet. I shuddered as I thought of it; he gave me so much pleasure.

Finally I began to think about my own thinking. I didn't think philosophically. This amused me. I could make no systems, advance no theories, just throw my-

159

self persistently against certain walls that would yield no meaning. I remembered a philosophy course I had taken in college, a survey of ways to think. I had learned to write essays that made me appear to be capable of thinking in different ways, it was a matter of style. But I didn't want to think in a *way,* I had concluded at the end of the course. I couldn't bear a coherent approach to myself or to other people. I didn't want to make order, and even the acceptance of chaos struck me as a dismal species of ordering. You don't want to think at all, I told myself.

The first rays of morning had paled the sky outside; the air was cool but still heavy, always heavy with damp. My pigeons began to stir in their cage. You're going to have to start thinking, I told myself. This idea made me so sad it was funny. I felt every cell in my body shrink away. Oh no, not that. I laughed. It's possible, I thought, to be mistaken about everything, about everyone. I could be completely wrong. Better to wait and see.

Maggie's drowsy voice silenced all this. "What time is it?" I turned to find her standing in the doorway, wrapped in my robe and the pleasant stupor of sleep. I was envious of her. She had lost everything and slept.

"Nearly four. Do you want something to eat? I made a casserole. It's really dull."

"If it's no trouble."

"It's in the oven. I just have to turn it on."

She sat down. "I am hungry."

I went into the kitchen and lit the oven. "What to drink?" I called to her. "Tea? Or maybe milk would be better."

"No, tea. Milk makes me sleepy."

"You can sleep all day tomorrow. You don't have to go to work."

"I have to go make some arrangements for Richard."

I joined her at the table with two glasses of tea. "Can't you get him out of there?"

"You mean altogether?"

"Sure."

"No. He burned a house down, and he acted crazy yesterday, and he continues to act crazy. The only place they'd let him out to would be jail."

"Is he . . . crazy?"

She smiled. "He was yesterday."

"You could tell?"

She nodded, averting her eyes from mine. "I could see it."

"Then you'll have to leave him there."

"I can't afford it. I don't have any insurance, I don't have anything now but what I make at work. And that's nothing."

"You can't let him go to Pineville."

"No."

"What about that place across the lake?"

"Mandeville?"

"Isn't it cheaper?"

"I think it is. A little. It's hard to get in there."

"And you'd never get to see him."

"I can't believe I'm responsible for him. I can't believe I'm responsible for this."

"For what?"

"Having made no provisions for anything."

"But you couldn't know."

She covered her face with her hands. "I knew," she said through her fingers.

"Have you ever been in a car crash?" I asked.

"No."

"There's a point when you know you're going to crash and you can see clearly, precisely what you could have done to avoid it. But you're past that, it's too late. And then you hear the noise."

She smiled weakly. "Last night, when he went in the bathroom, I saw his face, just a glimpse, as he was closing the door, and I knew. It was too late then, I knew that too. I didn't try to stop him."

"Had you been arguing?"

"We'd just made love. For the first time in weeks. It was a little frantic but exciting. I was lying in bed watching him and I was feeling quiet, exhausted. Then I saw his face. I think I didn't care."

"He didn't say anything?"

"No. He just went in the bathroom and closed the door. I heard him running water. Then I dozed a little. When I woke up I could hear burning, but I didn't know what it was, and crying, sobbing. I thought it was coming from the next apartment. I lay there for a few minutes. He started screaming all at once, as if he'd been stabbed."

"What was he saying?"

"Just screaming. You know, like a child screams. I jumped up and went to the door, but it was locked. There was smoke coming out from under it. I yelled to him to open the door and then he started screaming, 'Help me, help me.' I just threw myself at the door until the lock broke. The whole place was flames. He'd made a wall of

162

clothes, hung across the shower pole, piled on the floor, in the sink, and set them on fire. I could see him above the flames, sitting in the window, crouched in there, like a gargoyle. I thought, He's so small. He was screaming and waving his arms. 'Help me, help me.' I ran into the kitchen and got a broom, then ran back and lifted the clothes off the floor so I could get past. I threw them in the bathtub. Of course, the broom started burning. I don't know why I didn't think to turn on the shower. Then I grabbed him by the legs and started pulling him down. He was still screaming for help, but he fought me. The room was really hot, smoke everywhere. I kept thinking I was going to leave him and just run from the whole mess. But I fought with him until I got him out of the bathroom, and then I closed the door behind us."

"Did he keep fighting?"

"I don't remember too much after that. I think he did. At one point the neighbors were all swarming around; somebody brought me a sheet and I realized I'd been running around naked. I had my purse with me, I must have grabbed it on the way out. The girl in the back house gave me a dress. Then the fire trucks came—it took them a long time—and the ambulance. Richard was still screaming and crying, but there was so much noise going on no one seemed to notice him. They pulled him into the ambulance and I got in, too. They knocked him out with something right away. After that it was just people asking questions."

"Was he hurt?"

"His legs and hands were burned, but not too badly."

"You weren't burned?"

"I don't know how."

"Well," I said. "It's over now."

"That was the easy part, I think. The hard part comes now. The real shit."

"You can't try to be responsible for what he did."

"There isn't any way to avoid it. What's happened is what I've been avoiding for so long. Now it's done. The worst of it is, I really just want to wash my hands of it."

"If I can help you."

"You are helping me. You're not shocked by me?"

"No. Why should I be?"

"I think those doctors were. They were. They thought I was, I don't know, heartless, because I wasn't upset. They really gave me a bad time at Charity."

"What did they do?"

"They took Richard away immediately, as soon as we got there. Then they started firing questions at me. I said I didn't need to answer the questions because Richard wasn't going to stay there. They said I couldn't take him out until I got a doctor somewhere else. I got angry and this young doctor came out to calm me down. He gave me a shot. I didn't need a shot, I wasn't screaming, I was just trying to get someone to listen to me. I asked this guy to tell me what I had to do to get Richard out of there. He said the same thing: it couldn't be done unless I got a doctor to admit him somewhere else. So I said, 'Look, I don't know any doctors. Find me a doctor that can do this.' Then I talked to three others and finally I got a woman who called somebody at DePaul's. I kept filling out forms and everybody wanted to know what kind of insurance we had. I said I had it through work, I didn't know what company. But I don't. We could never afford it. Anyhow, it took all morning, and then they put Richard back in an ambulance and took him to DePaul's. He was still unconscious."

"You went with him?"

"No. They were so screwed up they didn't tell me they were going and I had to take a bus up there. Then when I got there they ran me around a little more. I never did see Richard; they'd taken him off somewhere. I haven't seen him since this morning. I keep thinking he must be dead. Or they've lost him somewhere." She paused. "I keep wishing that," she concluded. She covered her face with her hands, then shook her head, averting her eyes from mine. She pretended an interest in the pigeons, leaning away from the table to peer into their cage. "Will they ever lay eggs?" she asked weakly.

I followed her gaze. The birds were nestled close together, the male shielding the female's head against his chest. "They seem to like each other, but nothing comes of it," I said. When I looked back, Maggie had folded her hands on her lap and put her head down so that I wouldn't see the tears that streamed down her cheeks. I wanted to take her hand in my own, but even this small gesture struck me as too great an intrusion. I waited without speaking while she wept, quietly at first, then, resting her head on folded arms, in racking miserable sobs. After a long time she rubbed her eyes with her hands and said hesitantly, testing to see if she would be able to speak, "I'm sorry. I'm hysterical."

"Can you eat now?" I asked.

"Oh yes." She smiled. "I'm so hungry. I feel like I could eat and then sleep for a year."

I went to the kitchen and spooned some of the casse-

165

role into a plate. When I returned she was smoking a cigarette.

"I keep helping myself to everything," she said, pushing the cigarette pack away from her as if it were temptation.

I set the plate in front of her and resumed my seat. She ate voraciously, pausing only to assure me, "This isn't dull. It's good." When she was finished she pushed the plate away. "You haven't slept at all," she said. "You must be exhausted."

"No," I said. "I feel wide awake for some reason."

"I'm sorry to have barged in on you like this."

"I've been thinking," I said.

"I bet you have."

"I want you to stay here. I'm not trying to be nice or a friend or anything. I really want it. I want to see you through this . . . thing. I don't feel the least put out about it."

"I shouldn't," she said.

"It's hard to explain," I went on. "I think I knew this was going to happen too, it's something I've been waiting for. When you called me yesterday I felt relieved. And now, I feel . . ." I looked away. "I'm glad it's happened. I want to be involved in it. That's so unusual for me."

She appraised me curiously. "It is," she said.

I tried to cover for myself. "I've been having trouble sleeping," I said. "I can only sleep at Reed's. I think he's getting tired of that. If you were staying here, for a while, it might help."

"It hasn't helped tonight."

"It might," I finished lamely.

"I'm going to need all the help I can get," she said.

"Yours is the easiest to take." She frowned. "But I won't run you out of your bed."

"You can sleep on the sofa in the front. It opens up."

"Somehow I always thought it would be you who would have to call on me."

"I may yet," I said.

"Well."

"It's been a long time since we've had a chance to talk."

"Is everything all right with you?"

I told her of my conversation with Clarissa and my last encounter with Michael.

"What do you think he wants?" she asked.

"Whatever it is, I think he's given up."

"Suppose he comes back and I'm here."

"He won't come back."

"Does Reed know about it?"

"You mean what happened? Yes, he knows."

"What did he say?"

"Nothing. He's glad it's done. I think he was annoyed at how surprised I was."

"You're content with Reed."

"I don't want to say I am, but I can't say I'm not. He understands me. There isn't a lot of tension between us. I don't know, Maggie. A man? Is it a man I need? I just don't think so."

"No. I don't think so, either. Though there was a time when I thought if I couldn't have Richard I couldn't live."

"You were in love with him?"

"I was. I am. When I found out there were things about him that I didn't love, that I didn't know then, things I couldn't love, it didn't change anything. It doesn't change anything, it just makes it all so much more difficult. What I thought I loved in him, that's still there. When I saw him screaming for someone to save him from the disaster he'd brought on himself, I thought, I love him. That's what I love about him. He's so perverse, he wills things. He's not dead, like I think I am sometimes. I don't know. I thought he would love me, but he didn't. Toward the end there we were living two completely different lives, as if we'd never met. And I honestly couldn't tell if that wasn't the way it was supposed to be." She smiled, a sleepy, quizzical smile, like a child waking from a pleasant dream.

"How do you feel now?"

"Momentarily free. For the first time in a long time."

The room had slowly lightened, the air was cool, the sky a dull yellow and pink. My pigeons had begun rustling and cooing in their cage, a dog was barking somewhere. "Here comes the sun," I said.

"Could we take a walk?" Maggie asked. "I'd like to go out while it's still cool."

"Sure. We can do whatever we want." We left our dishes on the table and I went to search for my sandals while Maggie dressed quickly.

I met her on the front porch. She was sitting on the top step looking woefully at her feet. "I don't have any shoes," she said.

I sat down beside her. "What size do you wear?"

"Six."

"You can wear mine, then."

She wiggled her toes. "Not now, later. It's warm enough. I think I'd like to walk around without shoes."

We got up and began our walk. We talked about the

neighborhood. "I like it because it's so mixed up. There's a lot of little stores and I can get a bus downtown anytime."

"I liked living in the Quarter," she said. "It's convenient. But it's always the same people. Year after year. No one ever leaves."

We passed a young black girl sitting on her front porch. She was singing to herself, but stopped as we approached. "Why do you think she's up so early?" Maggie said.

"Maybe she's waiting for one of her parents to come home. Somebody who works all night."

"Are you going to go to work today?"

"I have to," I said. "I have some people scheduled. My supervisor will just put them off and they'll be twice as hot when I get back. I may leave early. The last one's at two."

"I guess I'll just go to the hospital and see what they say. Can I do anything? Go to the store? Wash clothes or something?"

"No. We need some milk. You could get that."

We continued our walk without talking, except to point out an interesting house or plant. Maggie noticed a heavy ripe cluster of plantains and we agreed that it would be nice to have such a tree. A late-blooming crepe myrtle caught my attention. "Why did it wait so long? Didn't it know it would get scorched?"

"It looks O.K. though," Maggie observed. The tree was small, its purple flowers dark and tight.

"I love this time of day," Maggie said as we turned the last corner to my house. "Everything is so still, you can smell the air. It's undisturbed."

169

"Yes," I agreed. "I feel better." We climbed the stairs and went inside. Maggie sat on the couch and plucked at her skirt.

"This dress is stupid," she said. "I would never buy a dress like this."

It was a sundress, with hundreds of little pleats across the bodice, wide shoulder straps, and a puffy skirt that would have seemed childish on anyone else. On Maggie it looked practical. "The material is nice," I said. "No wrinkles. The color is nice on you, too."

She sighed. "I guess I'll have to give it back."

"You can wear my clothes. We're about the same size."

"That's funny." She smiled, looking at me as if I were her reflection. "I never thought about it much before, but we are. I always think of you as smaller than me."

"No," I said. "I'm not. I never thought I was."

She laughed. "It's such a relief to me that you know I'm not crazy. You don't think I'm acting badly."

"You mean that I don't feel sorry for you."

"That too."

I grinned. "But I know how long you've waited, how long it's been on your mind that you were waiting."

"I guess that's it."

We busied ourselves in the kitchen, making more coffee. I fried an egg and ate some toast while Maggie sat smoking cigarettes. It struck me that we were like lovers, a little shy of each other, but each pleased by the other's presence. When I left for work she stood on the front porch until I was out of sight. I thought, Should she be left alone?—then reflected that I knew of no reason why she should not be.

✻ 9

As I got on the bus to work, it started to rain torrentially. I had no umbrella and settled myself into my seat with appropriate gloom; I would have to walk two blocks in a downpour and spend the morning drying out in air-conditioned discomfort at my desk. The people around me seemed to share my despondency, looking out the streaming windows without even the energy to make despairing comments. I knew from their faces that this was the early bus, the one I usually missed, and that I would arrive at work on time for a change. Then there would be questions about Maggie, about the fire. We had agreed that I would say it had been an accident and that Maggie could be expected to return in the next few days and explain it all herself. I decided to call her when I got to work to tell her where the umbrella was.

When I arrived I dried myself as best I could with paper towels. My shoes were soaked and squeaked when I walked. I drank a cup of coffee and discussed with a few other workers the possibility that the rain would keep clients away. We agreed that it would only make them all come in late and cantankerous. At my desk I glanced through the day's applications and called home. Maggie's hello sounded cheerful.

"I needs my food stamps today," I said. "Can you send them on over to me?"

She laughed. "Did you get soaked?"

"Yes. To save yourself that fate, use the umbrella in the kitchen closet."

"Thanks," she said. "Can I wear your red shoes? They fit. They go with this stupid dress, too."

"Sure. Why not wear one of my dresses if you're tired of that one? I don't mind, really."

"I might. These pleats are too much."

"Well, good luck," I said. "I may leave early. I'm getting sleepy already."

"Tell Joyce I'll call her this afternoon, and see if you can get me off the books for tomorrow."

"I'll try," I promised. We said goodbye, and as soon as I hung up the phone, it rang.

"Your eight-thirty is here," Kay informed me sleepily.

The morning passed uneventfully. My afternoon appointments both called to reschedule, so by 11:30 I had seen everyone I expected. I spoke to Maggie's supervisor and then to my own. Both assured me that Maggie's work could be handled and that my desire to leave early was acceptable. I ate lunch at my desk, made a few phone calls, and signed out at 2:00. Outside, the rain had stopped and the sun had come out blazing, so that the streets steamed and the sidewalk glared blindingly. I caught a bus right away and was home in fifteen minutes.

The house was empty. Maggie had washed the few dishes we had used and set them to dry in the rack. I

172

found a quart bottle filled with fresh tea in the refrigerator and poured myself a glass. I sat on the sun porch and put my feet up on the table. One pigeon was in his coop, the other had gone off somewhere. I talked to myself aimlessly, then gave in to a desire to sing. I sang a hymn I had heard at the Jazz Festival the year before. The refrain was "Throw out the lifeline, someone is drifting away." I didn't know most of the lyrics and wound up humming or simply repeating the few I did know. I felt contented with myself and matter-of-fact about my situation. When I had finished my tea and my song, I went into the front room and fell asleep on the couch.

I woke up when I heard Maggie at the door. I sat up sleepily as she came in and yawned. "You're back," I said.

She looked annoyed. "Go back to sleep," she said. "I didn't mean to wake you." I followed her through the house to the back room. She slipped my shoes off in the bedroom and shoved the umbrella back into the kitchen closet on her way.

"Is something wrong?" I asked.

She dropped into a chair at the table. "Do you know anything about these?" she asked. She drew two small green notebooks from her purse. Both were leather-bound, expensive-looking. I opened one and saw that page after page was filled with a thin, cramped red scrawl I recognized.

"These are Richard's," I said.

"Have you seen them?"

"Never," I said. "He wrote me a note once. I recognize the writing."

"You'd better read them."

"Now?"

"Right now," she said. "I've got nothing to do. I'll wait."

"Which is first?" I asked.

"The one that has your name written on top."

I opened one and saw my name slashed across the page in red. Beneath this I read, "I stand in the corner and beat my head against the wall." I looked up at Maggie. "Did he give these to you?" I asked.

"No," she said. "The shrink gave them to me. They were in his pockets."

I closed the book. "I don't think I should read this."

"You might as well," she said archly. "It's all about you."

"All right." I opened the first book again and began to read.

HELENE

I stand in the corner and beat my head against the wall. I can feel my brain recoiling, wary, afraid of the shock should I hit it as hard as it knows (it knows) I would like to hit it. I'd like to crack the bastard open.

Would anyone care to know what kind of man I am? I follow my wife's best friend, I am following her. That's what kind I am. I'm trying to find out something about her. I have a theory. I could explain myself by this theory. Or I could say that I am small and thin and sneaky and powerful. I've seen photographs of myself but I don't trust them. Mirrors were involved and mirrors put everything backward. What do I really look like? What is the look I have? Look at the woman I'm following, my expression is the opposite of hers. Where hers retreats, mine aggresses. Where her eyes soak up what she sees, mine are daggers that see only with intention. Where she is timid, shying away, pulling away, I am relentless. How can I describe myself? I've never seen myself.

174

When we sit across a table from each other, we have done that, then we exchange an awkward bolt of recognition that closes us in and everything else out. The rest of the world is nothing, everything is in that look. We've had it. And we both knew we'd had it. Most unusual, neither of us saw any need to deny that we had it, though we didn't talk about it. Circumstances don't permit us to talk.

How can I be sure? I am sure. I have all the evidence of my senses and hers.

She's afraid of everything but me.

My eyes, my ears, my nose, the skin on my face is sensitive, my tongue. All the senses concentrated in one little area. The head should be bigger. Our heads could be enormous but we don't see it that way. Seeing from our heads, we don't want to see it. Inside my head there is so much measurable space; outside, no limits. The reverse is also true. There is too much inside my head to be encompassed by inches. Every head I've ever seen contained a nightmare.

Helene is not like Maggie, thank Christ. Maggie has the disadvantage of being my wife. She can kiss me and if I don't respond she can get angry. I can't respond at all. Why should I? Is this a love affair? It's a marriage and a bad one. She is wanting, always wanting, wanting to know what I think, and watching me, watching me. Sometimes I don't even know what I'm thinking, I'm so busy trying to disguise it so she won't guess it. Do I owe her this? She can make me feel I do. She can make me feel, but only momentarily, that I have no right to my own thoughts. To my impulses, which are mine. But only momentarily.

I went to meet her at work one afternoon. This pleased her, to have me waiting for her when she got off. I had to sit in a waiting room with all the poor murderers on welfare, the humble poor, the faces you can't bear to look at, they are mindless, except for hate. I was only there because I knew how much it would please her to see me sitting out there with her beggars. She likes to think I'm one of them. I went to please her, no other reason.

And then I saw Helene. That was the first time I saw her. She was standing in the doorway. Everyone in the room looked up at her and most didn't look away. She stood with one hand pressed against the doorsill, looking down at some papers in her hand, looking up, her lips slightly parted, her breath sucked in, her head tilted back, her eyelids dropped a little over her eyes. She didn't look as if she would be able to see anything out of her eyes. She sees with her skin, but I didn't know that then.

A man stood up when he saw her and she recognized him. Her expression complicated. She saw the man and knew who he was and that he would speak to her, but he wasn't the man she was looking for. She stood in the door talking to him, pretending to be interested in him. I could see that he was gratified by the attention she was giving him, but all the while her back was stiff and she was waiting for someone else. Expecting someone else. She looked right at me over the old man's shoulder, but she didn't know me, we hadn't met then. She was new on the job, had been there two weeks. But she already knew how to do what she had to do, she knew how to handle the old man so that he was satisfied and she was untouched. She looked right at me, her eyes settled on my face without a trace of recognition. She was thinking, No, I don't know him. My eyes followed her when she was finished talking to the man, as she walked past me and spoke to the receptionist and then walked out of the room. My eyes were on her, didn't leave her. She felt my eyes on her, but since she didn't know me, she didn't care. What I saw. She didn't care then.

So for a long time it was easy to follow her.

When she and Maggie have lunch at LaForge, I can sit in the bar across the street and watch them in the patio. What does she see in Maggie? They talk for hours. Sometimes they take two hours for lunch. How does the department feel about that? And Maggie comes home and complains about her hard day. I say, "What did you do for lunch?" And she says, "Helene and I went to LaForge. Why?"

Why won't she bring Helene home, if she's so fond of her, if her secrets are so pleasurable? Doesn't she want her to see me and this place where she sleeps with me? Does she think her friend couldn't take it? Maggie is ashamed of me, afraid of me, she hasn't let herself in on it yet. She won't bring Helene home (where I might get my hands on her), and so I must sit at a bar and strain my eyes to see them, pretending I am not (they pretend, I pretend) even in this world.

I get tired of drinking, sitting in that bar watching them, pouring in liquids. Maggie eats bovinely and she never has more than two drinks. But Helene sometimes has three or four and she eats rapidly. I wish I could use binoculars but that would be too obvious. Maggie sits with her legs together and her elbows on the table. She can sit still longer than most people. She is capable of great deceit by keeping still. She has the attraction of carrion, of rotting flesh. Her presence would make a rock obsessive. I think she has some sense of how revolting she is to me. When she woke up that night with the tape around her head and I told her I was measuring her skull, she was terrorized because she knew if my measurements were accurate I would be on to her. I would find out the dimensions of the error that is rotting her.

She sits perfectly still in the restaurant, trying to cast her moribund fascination over Helene, like a snake charming a deer.

Helene waves her hands and smokes. She crosses and uncrosses her legs. She pulls her hands through her hair, pushes it back, then shakes it forward. She runs her finger up and down the side of her glass, cooling herself through that fingertip on the glass. She can concentrate all her attention on that one point, her fingertip against an icy glass, up and down. It drives people crazy to watch her. She's not fully conscious of anything, just her middle finger, up and down, rubbing the glass. She closes her whole hand around the glass and presses it so that she lifts it slightly from the table. She looks at her hand, leaving Maggie to gesticulate grotesquely, then sets the glass down, pulls her hand into her lap, and returns her attention to Maggie.

On whom everything is lost.

I press forward, she backs away, for the same reason. To cover for not being able to concentrate, for being able to concentrate too well. It's always there with her, at the back of everything: where am I, who am I talking to, what am I saying, is this talking, is this real, am I doing it right?

Heating the outside of the head has some effect on the brain. Sat in front of the gas stove for two hours. My forehead practically blazing. I could feel my brain being pushed around by the heat, expanding tight. Told Maggie I was going to take a bath. Plunged my head into hot water, body still in the cooler air, leaned over the side of the tub. Blood ran to head, head incredibly warm, body became completely numb. Sensation of well-being.

Later, on the street. Preret sees me. He looks away. He knows what damage I could do to him if I gave a damn. Slimy Preret. The abuse I took from him. I recall with satisfaction the day he came in and found me at my desk completing an obscene drawing of him and his secretary. "Haven't you got O'Reilly's job worked up yet?"

"You know, Preret," I say, "I'm not going to be able to do any more patios for you. No more concrete, no more palm trees. Just stuff like this. We'll have to change our whole line." I turn the drawing out for him to see. First he smiles, then recognizes the spread of his secretary's legs, his own impotent smile.

He was calm. It was Maggie who showed distress that I could no longer draw patios for Preret. No more patios, no more paychecks. I still think I should have murdered Preret. Or set fire to him. It would have been so easy. Everyone who ever met him wishes he was dead.

I am not totally without a sense of humor. Anyone can see that. There is no basis in fact for that accusation.

I didn't start following Helene at any particular time. I didn't know I was following her until after I had started. I think the first time was uptown. I was on a streetcar and I saw her walking on the sidewalk. I got off at the next stop in time to see her turning off St. Charles. I ran down the parallel street, and when I got to the corner I looked over and saw her crossing the street, turning left, toward me. There were banana trees up against a house. I stood in the midst of them. I thought she would see me. I tried to think of something to say. She walked right past me. I thought, Well, I'll follow her, since it's so easy. But even then I didn't know I was following her. I was just watching the way she walked, how straight her back is, the way her arms swing a little, and the way she never looks around. People passed her going the other way, she never looked to see if she might know anyone. When she got to her apartment she stopped and spoke to a man who was cutting the front lawn. She pointed to the back of the house. The man threw his arms up over his head. She laughed, said something again, then went inside without looking back. I was standing across the street. The man looked at me suspiciously, I was standing in plain view. I was sweating. I wiped my face on my sleeve and turned away, walked away in the direction I'd come from. I thought, I should be ashamed, but I wasn't. I felt exhilarated, my heart was beating rapidly, I had trouble catching my breath. There's a bar two blocks from her house. I went in there and drank until I calmed down. Then I went home.

What a case, what a case. A bunch of bones, skin on top. The softness of the thing, the thinking thing, soft as meat, tearable, chewable. It can rot right in the skull, it can rot like a fruit. Those of us who are in fear have the power of fear. Others sit and watch and don't move, nothing to move away from, nothing to move toward. But for those of us in fear it's important to stay in motion. Approach the fear. Move away from the fear. Approach the fear. Move away. We are in motion. We don't waste our time looking around, speculating. Helene and I. Moving toward each other, away from each other. Is she watching me? Is she waiting for me? She's waiting for me. Inside fear is love. Love of the thing we fear. Love for the fear, that sweet laugh. Can it harm me? Will it harm me? Can she harm me? Can she avoid harming me? This is love, who's afraid of whom?

I don't mean her any harm. What would I do to her if I could hold her still? I would kiss the back of her neck, press my mouth there at the soft nape of her neck, slip my hands beneath her blouse at the same time. I will have to feel her breasts against the palms of my hands. Is there any way to do that without her knowing? If she were unconscious? If I compressed her rib cage until she was unconscious?

She is never fully conscious. That's what I know about her. That's where we meet one another. She pulls away from me, wants to laugh at me. Oh, you're one, too? she thinks. Are you not really all here, too? When we were introduced I was a ride home for her, in my limping Ford. Maggie between us, "Helene, Richard, my husband." Those words stick in Maggie's throat. "My husband." And then Helene's look, her hand nearly proffered, then drawn away when our eyes come crashing together: Oh, are you one, too? She'd rather not take my hand, and for my part I am grinning insanely. Nervous Maggie, ashamed of me, sits between us on the car seat. And so I learned where she lives.

I get out of bed with red before my eyes. It creeps around during the night. Red in front of the eyes. Pain in hands. Continuous pain in hands. Dislike the sound of the cats. A cat comes into view. Dislike the sight of the cats. Repulsive stretching. Maggie stretches like that. Mews. Licks her hands. Curls up. Sleeps. But is never satisfied. She goes to work after breakfast. Alone I lean in corners, clean brushes, kick at cats. Restless, recollection of dreams, uneasiness.

I am the only person in the building. I could do anything. Could burn the place down.

Painted for six hours. I was fine. Excited, barely able to wait to get through it, to see what I'd done. Then I stepped back. There was a red and next to it a blue. Exactly right. Exactly as I thought. Completely unnatural. After a while I was very annoyed by the way they look. The red fine, the blue fine, but together? How to fix it. Change the colors? But they are the exact colors, they do exactly. It's just right. But something annoys me. I try to explain it to Maggie. She says they look fine. This annoys me. Maggie says if I don't like it I shouldn't hesitate to change it. Strong desire to slap Maggie when she says this. Strong desire to slap her.

I say, "Don't look at me like that." She says, "Like what?" I warn her. As I warn her I wonder, Why am I warning her? She no longer recognizes me, says, "It's unnecessary for you to warn me." I say, "One never knows."

We are enemies.

It is true that electricity is in the skin, that's what's measured in lie-detector tests. Sometimes there is more than other times. Lying makes electricity. So does fear. The night I found Helene in the bar, she was playing chess. She plays badly, it's not a game for people who live by their nerves. Then I had her. It was easier than the first time. She thought I was drunk and so she thought I didn't know. But I wasn't drunk. (I'm never drunk.) I wanted to get her alone and tell her, but not to tell her is so important, since she knows. Then, in the cathedral, she was under my power. It shocked me. What could I have done to her?

But I'm waiting for the exact right time when her skin will be most electric. When her skin is so electric with fear that she gives off light. (I can see the light of fear.) Then will be the time. I can't decide how to take her. It must be sudden.

On the street the power left me, lifted like a hand, and she felt it go and tried to have contempt for me. When I pressed her against the wall I had a little power, enough. I pressed her hands against the wall. She turned her head and I saw a line of light run from her ear to the base of her neck. I touched that place but it was gone. Would she struggle? She thought I would kiss her; to hell with that. I pushed away from her and left her there on the street. We must get the timing exactly right. I like the idea of the cathedral floor. Sacrilege would be a joy to me if it were that, but the place is a tourist house at best. But the cold floor and the ceilings, the smell of the place. I can feel how it would be there.

Sat in front of the gas burner, burning nonsensically. My mind wandered, settled on Helene, conjured a monumental passion. In the midst of it, suddenly, fire sprang up, burned furiously, and when I gave up my imagining, it settled as quickly as it had begun and was gone. Fire would be the first symptom I would project upon the external world if the power takes over.

There are five steps to Helene's front porch. She was on the third. The man was on the first. That was how they were when I drove up. I parked across the street so I could see them in the rearview mirror. They were talking. I could see that she wasn't pleased with what the man was saying. She answered him, then bit her nails while he talked. Then she followed him to the curb and watched him get in the car. She stood on the curb and watched him drive off. I was so close I could see the expression on her face. She looked after the car wearily, she was tired of the man (who is he?), exhausted by him. Then her expression changed and what I saw froze me where I sat. She rubbed one side of her face with her hand, then let her head drop back, looking up into the burning sky with such pleading, such pain, I thought the sky must open for her, answer her. What has hurt her? Was it the man (who is he?)? I couldn't bear it, had to look away. I studied my aching hands. When I looked again she hadn't moved, and I said, "Stop, please stop," but she didn't hear me, didn't see me. She turned away without looking over to see who was sitting in a parked car across the street from her house. She never looks at things like that. Lucky for me, then, I couldn't have spoken.

I've been following her for some time now and still she hasn't seen me. I followed her to the city limit a few weeks ago. All through town and out the Vets Highway, out into Metairie, all the way to the new interstate. But I stopped there. I can't leave the city. Even to follow her, I can't leave the city. There are some things I will not do. If I leave the city, I'm lost. When they try to destroy me, when she tries to destroy me, she'll tell them to take me out of the city. They'll take me across the lake. That will be the end of me.

Does she know I'm following her?

There was a breeze that day when she was standing on the curb talking to the man, to that man, the one who so worries her. It blew her skirt up and she pushed it down. She didn't care much, she would have let it fly up, she was in such pain, but she has good reflexes. I know that. I've noticed that. Her reflexes are good. When I followed her to the city limit, a car came between us and cut in front of her, nearly ran her off the road. She didn't reduce her speed. She didn't want to. She didn't need to, she knows her reflexes are good and she can rely on them to pull her out. She doesn't ever have to slow down for anything. She's like me. She drives that bastard Reed's car; is that why she spends so much time with him? She doesn't care if she wrecks his car. Why should she?

She pushed her skirt down without thinking about it and really only held one side down so that the other side puffed up and I saw, in the rearview mirror, the upper part of her thigh, even a touch of blue that must have been silk, the softness of that color. Her legs are pale, I noticed that the first time I saw her. I could see the veins in her ankles. I could count them if I could get her to hold still long enough. And the veins in her thighs and around her nipples, in the backs of her knees and on the insides of her elbows. And in her hands.

Then she went back into her house without looking back. She never looks around. She doesn't want to see me. She is content to feel me watching her. And I am content to be felt. When I am watching her, I can feel her with my eyes, and feel that she knows she is being touched by my eyes, as surely as she is touched by the railing as she passes, and by the door-knob and by the sheets of her bed. Some women have one sense to rely on. Their eyes are useless to them. It's the sense of touch with them. That's all they have. That's all she has.

How does she feel about being touched by me? She doesn't mind. She was made for it.

I dreamed of fire this morning. No people, just fire. Woke up, thought I saw the curtains start to flame. How does a curtain burn? Like a woman's hair. Hang her upside down, a woman would burn like a curtain. Hair burns all at once in a flame, like a bad idea. Sat up in bed. No fire.

Not enough space inside my head. The place is crowded.

Fear is certain to start pressing out, fill the room, animate externals. I thought the curtain was burning.

Then I went out into the street. Terror on the stairs. Heard something behind, then below. Ran out into street in a sweat. Ran to Jackson Square. People everywhere. Went into cathedral. Repulsive smell, depressing statues in corners. Blood everywhere. Passed the confessional. Passed the confessional.

183

Went inside. Listened for the priest, looked through the little hole. There's his nose. I said, "I'm afraid I'm going to kill an animal."

Slow inhalation of breath from the other side. "How long?"

Does he mean since my last confession? Or how long the fear? Stand up, back out, run for the street. In a real panic now. Run across the square. Try to stay in public.

Who is she? Helene. If you can't see me, can you see her? When she goes out on the street, she is being followed and she feels it. Not just by eyes that settle on her back for a few moments, by strangers' eyes that speculate about her as she passes, noticing her eyes, presuming her to be as vacant as she looks. But by my long, patient, and intense consideration, by my long-suffering eyes. I have almost lost my life following her, through traffic, through crowds, walking as blindly as she walks. Our lives have been endangered together.

On the street I'm the only one no one follows. And I'm following Helene. We're getting a good look at me.

It's hard to keep up with her. She went into the hospital and I sat outside on the steps, in plain sight, waiting for her. Have you noticed how often I'm in plain sight? She doesn't see me. She came out a little while later, came down the steps in a daze. I could have jumped up in front of her and she wouldn't have seen me.

Maybe there are two kinds of love, at least two kinds, and one puts its object far away, beyond touch, beyond hope, and the other turns into its object. And both could happen at once, couldn't they? don't they? and when they happen both at once to two at once, it's power, it's historical. People have loved blindly, haven't they? isn't that what they say? They say the two don't see one another's faults, they don't have any faults for one another, they are all in all one another's faults. And that's why one sees that the other is a weakness. And that's what Helene sees about me. I am her weakness incarnate. How could she resist? And she is my weakness. We push each other away, beyond touch, beyond hope. If we were to touch, hope would be lost. If we were to really touch.

I am ready to abandon hope. I can give up. I have the power

to give up, the power of fear and the recognition of weakness and an identity I would be glad to give up, glad to get rid of, glad to lose.

And she is nearly ready. A little more. She'll be ready. I can hardly wait.

It would be burning and drowning all at once. Drowning in blood that is on fire. Fire like blood.

Transparence. Opaqueness. Seeing through and not being able to see through. Water is both. Fire is both. Paint, unfortunately, is both and neither.

I'm not just a man who wants to be noticed by a woman who's not noticing him. This is more subtle than that. Other men see her on the street and feel that, a shallow emotion, they want her to notice them because she's immune. They would like to do something to her, shake her up, open her eyes, startle her. They would never follow her as I do, patiently, good-naturedly, feeling the ebb and flow of power, electricity between us. It's better now that she knows who I am, that we've spoken, that she knows. That the way she feels with me is the way she feels when she's alone.

Or thinks she's alone and I am behind her somewhere.

Following.

Closing in on her.

This is a way to see her. This will be the last way to look at her. A letter, in the dark. She finds it under the door. Opening her door after work. I am on the street, watching. Walking into her empty apartment alone. She throws down her purse, flips a light switch, steps out of her shoes, turns . . .

There's an envelope on the floor.

She picks it up, holds it. She's frightened. So frightened she can't open it. Cannot open it. She turns it over and sees her name written there.

And she thinks, Is this it?

Have you decided about your face yet? Do you think you know how it looks? How it looks when you're reading? You know if your mouth's open. You know how it looks when what you read makes you smile. Now right before you smile there's a moment you don't know about in which you wouldn't even recognize your own face, it's that filled-with-terror second, right before you smile.

When Maggie opens a book I'm filled to the limit with murderous rage.

I don't believe the failure at the cathedral was my fault. She was numb. I saw it when she turned into the alley. I was standing against the wall across from the cathedral door and I know she saw me. She went inside, I was supposed to follow. Why couldn't I go in? I had two shocks. The first went from the base of my skull to the top of my head, the second went from ear to ear, as if I had a live wire between my teeth. I put my hands over my ears. I wanted to see her, but if I had another shock in front of her, I was afraid I might hurt her. Though she wouldn't respond as Maggie does, with cringing sympathy. She would only look at me with that detached surprise, almost amusement but for the fear. Someday some man will beat her senseless for that look. But not me, I can't hurt her. I don't want to frighten her. I am incapable of hurting her. That's why I've determined on her. But after those two bad shocks I was too nervous to follow her inside. And I had seen her face, she wasn't receptive. Her skin was dull, no charge to it. So the failure was partly my fault, partly hers. She could have stopped it all if she had spoken to me when I followed her to the cab. Why did she look back? I felt as if her eyes made me fall away, fall back. I was only what she saw, a man turning back, falling away.

She would like to find a spot in the center of everything where everything would whirl around her like the center of a symphony, a pitch off which every other sound reverberates, the color every other color has to go through, not being any color at all. There are times when she sits in my head like that, at the very center. Every thought would like to displace her, every idea is a reason to pretend she isn't there, but there, for a second, she sits.

Sometimes one full immeasurable second.

Not having any of the senses that show in every move she makes, I envy those senses being in her. She has balance, proportion, a queer unpremeditated grace. I saw her trip once on the street; a piece of sidewalk was broken and the heel of her shoe caught in it. Her ankle twisted, the heel of her foot came out of the shoe, every muscle in her body hurried to correct this mistake, all expression drained from her face. Her hands didn't fly up, her knees didn't buckle beneath her, she didn't stumble awkwardly exclaiming with high-pitched exasperation as some women do. She corrected her balance and without a sound she was on her way.

Did she ever really know she had done this? Did she think, I nearly fell there? Would she recall later that she had nearly lost her shoe, say, when she took that shoe off in the evening?

She didn't. She never knew what she did, what I saw then. I was across the street, standing behind a tree, and I saw the whole thing.

Surely you know there are times when it's strange to be alive. Your pulse beats, you know you're breathing, you can look out of your eyes and see where you are, locate yourself, but still it's strange. Is it quiet? But from somewhere you can hear, scarcely hear, something else living making a sound. Or is the sound coming from inside you, your own head?

The noise of human bodies makes me sick. When I pull my hair I can hear my heart beating at the roots. There are always too many sounds near me. My hearing is acute. I can hear everything. The refrigerator hum. I can hear Maggie's breathing all the time. I look for a quiet place but there are none. I can hear a roach moving down the wall in the next room. I can hear the sound a lizard makes, puffing up his red throat.

I have the feeling of being very heavy. Sometimes I feel light, then all at once very heavy. My hands hurt constantly. My gums bleed. Sometimes I feel shooting pains inside my stomach and up my back. I can't eat, I rarely eat. The worst pain of all is head pain. Low in the back of the head and drumming behind the eyes. Eyestrain. Too much looking out. Looking out too hard.

The word "island" makes me uncomfortable. I paint a woman on a chair in a circle, the circle is an island. Around that I allow a void.

187

I knew where she was today, I was ready to see her. On the stairs I kept forgetting. I keep forgetting. Not her face, it's with me, but how to get to her. What is the way to get to her? When we talked, once, she smiled. She looked away still smiling at me, about me, and I was by her side. And when she left in the cab she looked out and saw me. I felt her eyes on my back. She is looking for me. I do not doubt that she will find me now that I am so weak and keep forgetting everything in my brain which is lost in my head and on fire she is finding me. Will she find me in time?

Trouble focusing eyes, a stabbing pain in right eye, stabbing into the brain. Spiritual dryness, emotional narcosis. I can sit for hours dangling my hands, for hours, it means nothing to me. Maggie inquires about my mythical search for employment. I talked to some people on the street, something will break soon. Everyone says so. She believes this.

I'm too thin. The skin is wasting on my bones. I can see the bones in my wrists. The skin on my skull is thinning out. Especially around my eye sockets. And over my forehead.

The veins in a leaf are like the veins in a hand. Inside the stalks of big plants liquid runs up and down, just as it does in the stalks of people. Everyone knows this, but no one sees how dangerous it is. There's electricity on plants and on people, in the skin. It's energy escaping. It runs all over the skin, makes it powerful, electric. Skin has voltage. Skin can generate power. My skin is thinning out and the voltage is getting higher, I can feel it. Helene has a high voltage. She tries to control it, but I don't think she'll succeed. She'll give way to the power she is generating and it will bring her to me.

Maggie has no electricity. She is burned out. I burned her out, but it's her own fault, because that's what she wanted. Her imagination was never more than a thumbnail. And her love for me was, is, morbid curiosity. She would enjoy seeing animals tortured. She kills insects with gusto, thinking it's me she's grinding into the linoleum with her heel. The way she looks at me when I come in every day with my skin a little tighter on my skull and the electricity. She gives me a smile that disguises vomit; she would vomit up her sickening fear and revolting morbid curiosity if she hadn't learned to smile like that. I could slap her until she bleeds. She dreads the sight of me, what satisfaction, scrutinizing me with dread as if I might disclose a clue. I *am* a clue, there are no clues in me.

Always before sleep I have a sensation of color coming up around the sides of my face. I look to one side and then to the other. And there is the edge of the color. Usually some shade of red, sometimes blue. Can't sleep, waiting for this color to catch up with me. I wake up and walk through the rooms and look at these things that I've made and I know that I would have been better off making anything else than these things. I would have been better off without color, without eyes.

I dislike the kitchen. When I go in there I can feel the food all around me.

My face in the mirror. There is the face and there are the things that are not the face. Don't like the look of the eyes. Do I look like that? There is the area inside my head. How is it shaped? Is it really sealed in with skull? What kind of edge is in there? Does the brain run right up against the edge of the skull? Or is there some kind of cushion in between? Must get a medical book. No wonder everyone suffers from headaches. Is there anyone who hasn't had one? With all that inside. With everything inside. I dream that blood comes pouring out of my ears. I am talking or walking somewhere, or in bed with someone, and then I put my hands over my ears and blood gushes out between my fingers.

And I can't see. It's my sight running out. It's myself.

She's still important to me. A lifeline. I hang on, but the truth is, I'm gradually less concerned with the line and more concerned with the rising water around me. Still I hang on, hardly even conscious of her. I should have caught her in the church and held her down on the floor and driven through her. She wouldn't have screamed. She trusts me, why else would she have come? Why didn't I go to her?

After she left in the cab I went to a number of bars and then I went home. Maggie awake, reading one of her books. She puts her book down to look at me. What is this interruption? Then sees it's me and looks curious. She isn't curious, she just makes that face. She doesn't like having her reading interrupted, but then I am crazy, likely to do anything, have to be watched. Are you all right? she asks. How to answer? I lean against the wall. She gives me her most indulgent smile. Did you drink a lot?

If she had the courtesy to be angry, would it be easier to take? If she could put down her book without reluctance? She's hoping to find what's wrong with me in there, she thinks; if she could just understand, she thinks.

She looks at her book. Do I know the meaning of the word "formication." It's right there in her book. In my ignorance I do not. She shows me, I look at the word, I don't like it. What could it mean? She says it refers to the sensation of ants crawling across the skin. There would be a word for that. She says, "Sounds like 'fornication.' That's what it might be in this place, in this play. Probably the audience mistakes it, thinks the man says 'fornication' when what he refers to is ants crawling across the skin." Why would anyone think up such a word?

I don't see the point of going on with this. I don't know why we live together. I tell her that. I just distract you from your books.

She puts her book down seriously, puts it away from her. See, I'm not interested in that book. "What do you want me to do?" she asks.

I can't say what she expects me to say: "I want you to leave." Why not? I don't want to go into my studio because of the paintings in there. I can't stand the kitchen, I can hear the food. The bedroom is out, she'll follow me and sit on the bed, longing for some serious talk. There's the bathroom, my prison, the ten square feet she and Helene have left me. I can write in my books, run the water, try not to notice that I am not going to be able to hang on to Helene much longer. So, what next? What next?

Why did she just let me follow? Why not run or turn and face me? She knew it was a mistake but did it anyway. When I went to meet her I didn't believe I'd sent that note. I'd walked up to her apartment and shoved it under the door. All the neighbors saw me, through their curtains. They will all say, besides whatever else they want to kill me for, that I was following that poor young woman. I lurked about her apartment, I shoved bombs under the door.

I'm about to become a criminal.

If you lose your mind, no one will care. It will be what they expected. They'd all rather see you go under than watch the struggling. Can my mind be lost in my head? Am I losing track of its location in my head?

Headache. Trouble focusing eyes, head feels arid, dry, nose and throat hurt, knees are very weak, hands tremble. Difficulty holding pen. The worst is the trouble focusing my eyes. I've had it since I beat my head in the corner. Did I break something then?

It's getting harder and harder for me. I know what I am. I know what's at the heart of me. It's harder and harder to keep from seeing it. I try to paint what I see. That's all. Can anyone else see it? Is it morbid, can it be seen, doesn't she see it? Does anyone else feel this way?

I feel a choking sensation as if my throat were closing, at the same time queasiness in the stomach, and in the chest the fluttering helplessness that weakens knees after a nightmare. I am awaking from a bad dream which I am on the verge of falling back into. Hallucinations, untranslated, unresolved. In the next second, should I turn, I can hear them falling into place behind me; should I turn, will I be able to turn back? The cats are about to speak, the table is about to collapse, the windows are about to come smashing in, the walls to crack, the mirror to shatter, the plants to attack me, the floor to open, the blood to pour out of my nose and ears, my hands to write a language I don't recognize, if I look up from my page my vision will split. Am I standing behind myself watching, waiting for the pen to stop? If I look, won't I see my reflection in the mirror behind me, watching myself, waiting? Whose hand is this? what words are these? How can I control them, what form they take, if I should sink my teeth into my arm, I want to stop and not entertain this. Yet to control it, a force moves around me. Inside, the fears retreat before the power and the

191

power is a vision in blood. What am I hanging on to? is it her reflection? My own hands delude me, would kill in spite of me, would destroy me. I fear to be alone, with myself, with someone else, with the power. When the power comes it comes over me. I am not anything but the power which consumes me, I give way. Can I stop this? Let me stop this. I give way. Why is there no mercy in it, can't I be saved from this? They fear me, will not stop me. I've begged her and she knows it, but has no mercy, turns away, gets into a cab, looks at my back, the back of my flaming head. My head burns inside, my tongue burns in my mouth, throbbing in my ears, the sound of fire. Why can't I be saved as well, why is there no mercy for me? I'm in here. I'm in here. I'm in here.

I stop. I hold my breath, turn, and render the horror behind me into a harmless room. I can control my hands and I can see myself.

I can see my whole experience as a history of treachery, others against myself.

Everyone is interested in the motives of one who commits a crime, an atrocious crime, after it's committed. The more atrocious, the more interested the world becomes. But if you live in unremarkable darkness and never scream—who hears? Can you hear yourself?

Of course she will betray me. Why shouldn't she? She has herself to think of. But she knows and will come too late.

So this is it. This is how it happens. I didn't think it would be like this. I didn't think I would know. I can see what I'm doing. Sometimes I even have time to leave the room, go into the bathroom so Maggie won't see, stand in front of the mirror, and scream with no sound. I have time, pure lucid moments, time to hide myself.

A woman can destroy me, a woman like that. She surrenders, she can't help but surrender, she can destroy me. I don't wish to harm her but she would let me and so I would. Against my wishes, I would.

This is the beginning of everything. I have arrived at a place no one cares to hear about, though everyone will want to know what I did to get here.

I did these things to avoid getting here and these other things once I had decided, To hell with it, go ahead. I tried Helene but it was a failure. She holds out her hand but withdraws it when we would touch, and if we should touch I fear I might kill her. I tried painting, but I was painting the inside of my head a tolerable color. I haven't the courage to paint in the colors that are drowning me. I tried some measurements, solid evidence of the outside. There are several ways to measure the skull. Water displacement, this gives you the volume. Difficult to manage alone. I succeeded by oiling the water and measuring where the line was after I had, so carefully, immersed my swelling cranium. Underwater the head is as quiet as death. Another method, calipers, carefully constructed, to measure the circumference of the three ellipses that constitute the skull, then a formula which leads to a meaningless number.

I can feel my pulse everywhere. If I make a fist with my hand I can feel it in my thumb. If I rest my head against my forearm I can hear it throbbing, regular, loud. If I lie on my back I can feel it in my stomach and my fingertips. If I close my eyes I can see it in red on my eyelids. It's getting stronger. It throbs at my temples. I think it must be visible when I'm talking. I can feel it in the roof of my mouth, just behind my teeth. I'm pulsing. It's painful.

Absolute clarity of intention. The pursuit of absolute validity of intention. Intentional pursuit of absolute clarity. Of course there's a point of intersection. Of course every line intersects every other line at some point in every conceivable plane. I am not any nearer to anything by being afraid of everything.

I am afraid of the color red
I am afraid of the ellipsoid
I am afraid of the shape of the mind, of any speculation
about the shape of the mind
I am afraid of the word *decay*
I am afraid of cancer
I am afraid of a brain tumor

I am afraid of the color black
I am afraid of my wife
I am afraid of the word *microcosm*
I am afraid of the word *transformation*
I am afraid of the staircase
I am afraid of the closet
I am afraid of the sound in the pipes
I am afraid of my reflection
I am afraid of my reflection
I am afraid of plants
I am afraid of knives
I am afraid of breaking glass, of the sound of breaking
glass
I am afraid of closing and opening doors
I am afraid of the points where the walls meet, especially
the corners of the ceiling
I am afraid of answering the door
I am afraid of drowning
I am afraid of water
I am afraid of fire
I am afraid of being buried alive
I am afraid of smothering in my sleep
I am afraid of being smothered in my sleep
I am afraid of the word *deranged*
I am afraid of the tapping in the walls
I am afraid of my reflection
I am afraid of turning out lights
I am afraid of my own hands
I am afraid of cats
I am afraid of rodents
I am afraid of dogs
I am afraid of the tapping in the walls
I am afraid of water
I am afraid of my own hands
I am afraid of ants
I am afraid of ants

❋ *10*

The first notebook, which was almost entirely devoted to me, shocked me so that from time to time I simply let my eyes wander across the page, pretending to read, afraid to let Maggie see my face. In some places the handwriting looked as if it had been strangled and I had to strain to make it out. Maggie got up and walked about the room. As I began the second book, she said she would make some coffee and went into the kitchen. I put the book down and rested my head in my hands. I felt as if Richard were standing at my shoulder. "So this is what it was about," I wanted to say to him. "Why didn't you tell me?" I felt as I had felt once before, when a professor I had had in college, a man I had always admired, shot himself. On learning of his death I thought, If only I had known. If it was only someone to want him that he needed, I would have wanted him. But Richard was still alive and, I thought, anything I said about what I found in his notebooks would betray him. How could I tell Maggie this? As I finished the second book, she set a cup of coffee in front of me and sat down at the table. I drank it without looking up, the notebooks placed carefully face down before me.

"Well?" Maggie said after a moment.

I touched the books with my fingertips. I felt they might burn me if I said the wrong thing.

"I didn't know anything about this, any of this," I said.

"That's hard for me to believe," Maggie said. "You've already admitted he wrote you a letter."

"It was a note. Telling me to meet him."

"And you did."

"I went to the cathedral. He followed me when I came out. We didn't talk. But that's in here." I tapped the notebooks with my forefinger. "That was the first time I had any idea he was following me."

"Did you have lunch with him?"

"Once. That was some time ago. It was innocent enough."

"Not innocent enough to tell me about it."

Her tone annoyed me. "I'm not going to try to defend myself to you. What would you have done if I'd said, 'Your husband is bothering me'?"

"Then you don't deny that what's in those books is true?"

"It's all true," I said. "I wish he had seen me less clearly. But where does it say I encouraged any of this?"

"Does he have power over you?"

I met her gaze. "No," I said. "Honestly, none at all. That's why he says I failed him. You can see that."

She turned away, covering one cheek with her palm so that I wouldn't see the expression on her face.

"I never touched him," I said. "Except that day we had lunch, he took my arm. But other than that . . ."

"This isn't a matter of touch," she interrupted. "This is a matter of possession."

"I never wanted to possess him."

"Are you sure?" she insisted.

"He was an annoyance to me."

She allowed me a moment's silence in which the pretentiousness of this statement was resonant. "I just can't believe it," she said. "I was resigned to letting him go, if he had to go, wherever it was he was so intent on going, away from me. If I couldn't go with him, then I was willing that he should go. I could give him up to himself. But to find out that it was someone else, that it was you. That he thought so little of me." She paused. "What he says about me in there isn't true. I can't see myself that way. It's simply not what happened."

I could think of no reply.

"When I went to that hospital today, I felt like I was in control of things at last. I thought he couldn't hurt me now, that nothing he could do would ever be directed at me again. I had to sit in a little room and talk to this horrible man, the shrink. He wanted to know all about me, all about Richard. He asked the most dreadful personal questions. I said things like, 'I can't talk about that.' And of course he said, if I wanted to help Richard, I was just going to have to make this terrific sacrifice and talk about things that might not seem relevant, that might seem none of his business. I wanted to say, 'Look, he's gone. Nothing I can say will help him now.' But I just kept trying to get around it. I wanted to talk about money, about how in hell I'm going to pay for this. But he said that would be a matter to discuss with the business office. The business office!" She laughed harshly, glancing at me to make sure I saw the absurdity of this. "Then he gave me these notebooks. He said he found them in Richard's pockets and that I should see them, but that he would want them back. I don't even know if *he*'s read them yet." She reached for the notebooks, then pushed them a little farther away. "I'm not giving them back."

"No," I agreed. "You shouldn't."

"Do you think we should destroy them?"

I didn't want her to see how much I objected to this idea. I touched the books casually. "I don't know. Not right away."

"When I read them I was so angry. So hurt."

"Did you see Richard? Does he know you have them?"

"No. They said he was too sedated. I can see him to-morrow."

"Will you tell him about these, that we have them?"

"I don't know. It depends on what kind of condition he's in."

I tried to imagine how the notebooks must look to her. "Maggie," I said, "I would have told you. I wasn't watching that closely. This mess with Michael, I've been so involved in it. And whenever I talked to you about yourself, you didn't seem to want me to know anything. So I was trying to keep out of it. I thought that was what you wanted."

"I don't know what I would have done if you had told me," she admitted. "It wouldn't have made any difference. It's just these books, the way he writes in these books. I feel I should have had some clue and it makes me angry. I can't imagine writing things like this, thinking like this. It's alien to me and I was living with it."

I nodded agreement, though I didn't agree. I was

queasily conscious of how the writing had struck me. It wasn't alien at all. I had felt from start to finish a persistent lucidity, so that even as one part of me responded, This is madness, this is confusion, another followed the sentences with a sense of righteous satisfaction; yes, this came first, this was the obvious conclusion of that. "It's not me," I said. "You can see that. It's some idea he had about me, something that I meant to him. But I never was. I never was anything to him. He imagined it."

She considered this. "Why you?" she said. "That's what I keep wondering. Of all people, why you? Did he know that turning to you would hurt me most?"

I thought I knew why Richard had chosen me and I didn't think Maggie had anything to do with it. I could feel him, across town, sitting in a small white room, being observed by strangers, eating hospital food, waiting for nothing. I wanted to see him, to tell him I knew and had not meant to fail him. I listened to Maggie halfheartedly. She was in the center of it all now; she had complete control over his fate, and this pleased her. In fact, now that she had this power over him, I could see that she could no longer remember when she had not had it. So she thought Richard chose me because of her. I didn't try to dissuade her from this reasoning, there was no point in that. I would let her think what was most useful for her to think, and in the morning, I decided, I would go to the asylum and try to see Richard.

We talked for the rest of the evening. I told Maggie all I knew about her husband, all that had passed between us, and I tried to explain my own motives in keeping this information from her. I was surprised myself to hear what these motives were. As I drew out each one, em-

199

bellishing it with an awareness I knew I simply had not possessed at the time, I began to wish I couldn't hear myself. But Maggie believed me and concluded at last that there was nothing either of us could have done to avert the present disaster. She was convinced that Richard had chosen his fate, pointing to his misguided writings as proof. I made a weak defense for him. "There's such a difference between wanting to be able to lose control and then losing it," I said. "There must be some point he just slipped past."

"Possibly," she said. She didn't want to discuss it.

Maggie went to bed early and I sat on the sun porch for a while musing hopelessly. I thought of Richard, and of the effort he had made to reach me. What Maggie saw in his journal was only his intent. What I felt most was his reluctance. He had not wanted to follow me, he had not wanted to write what he had written. Did he think if he didn't believe what he wrote that he was somehow safe from it, from having written it? Who has not felt that? Hadn't I dismissed my pathetic letter to Michael for the same reasons? No one, I thought, goes mad for love of madness. It was something irresistible and irreversible, a process so distasteful one could only try to ignore it until it was too late. Was I ignoring evidence of madness in myself? The thought didn't make me eager to attempt sleep. I smoked cigarettes and sat gazing before me for hours. Toward dawn I went to bed and slept until seven.

Maggie got up shortly after and we ate breakfast quietly. Richard's notebooks lay between us on the table, but neither of us acknowledged their mute presence. I wanted to open them, read them once more, but I resisted the temptation because I didn't want Maggie to know how they fascinated me. Maggie said she planned to try to see Richard about ten, she wanted to spend the morning on the phone trying to determine how expensive his treatment would be and how she could pay for it. I promised to call her from work later in the day to see how she had fared.

When I left the house she stood on the porch again and I waved to her as I rounded the corner. I took a different bus than my regular one, this one to the end of Magazine, where I caught another that brought me to within three blocks of the hospital. It was eight o'clock when I stopped at a phone booth to call my supervisor and tell her I would be late and that I wasn't expecting any clients. She wasn't in yet herself, so I left my message with the switchboard. Then I walked to the hospital.

I had often passed the place before without paying much attention to the forbidding façade. A ten-foot brick wall surrounded the entire block, above this neo-Gothic arches lined the long barred windows that were visible from the street. I had to walk halfway around the block before I found the iron gate. I was relieved that Richard was here and not at Charity, where I knew I would not have dared to look for him. My clients referred to the mental ward there simply as "the third floor," and when members of the family found their way there, they were thought of as irredeemably lost, as if they had fallen into a hole in the earth. In spite of its medieval appearance, DePaul's had a more civilized reputation. The man who opened the big iron gate for me didn't appear to be the least demented. I didn't look around once I got into the building. I would not be distracted from my mission.

I went through a series of rooms, and spoke to several

people. I told each one my name and explained that I wanted to see Richard. The first was a woman and she said it would be impossible. The last was a man, Richard's psychiatrist. He invited me to sit in a chair and tell him why I was there.

"I want to talk to him," I said. "I'm a friend of his. I want to see him."

"Why don't you sit down?" he said, seating himself in a chair that would face me if I did as I was told.

I stepped back and leaned against the door. "It's important to me," I said.

"But why? Are you related to him?"

"He wrote something. Something about me. I have to talk to him about it."

"What did he write? A letter?"

"I don't want to talk to you about it," I said. "I want to talk to him."

"I'm afraid you have to talk to me first."

I looked away from him, biting my lip. My eyes settled on his diploma, which was hanging on the wall behind him. I looked back at his face, a bland frozen mask of skin topped with fiendishly curly hair, and he saw that I saw there only an obstacle. "Don't do this to me," I said.

"What am I doing?"

"Will you let me see him or won't you?"

"I can't say. I don't know enough to say. I'm waiting for you to tell me why I should."

"Is he a prisoner here?"

"Why are you so defensive? You know the circumstances of his being admitted."

"I know he was brought here against his will."

"I'm not responsible for what he did. But I am responsible for what he does while he's here. Why don't you sit down?"

"I don't have that much time. I have to go to work."

"Is he your lover?"

I could feel my face flushing with rage, and I was sure he saw it.

He smiled. "You seem so urgent."

I wanted to flee the room, but my determination to see Richard got stronger as my anger increased. I went to the chair and sat down. I knew that if I had been carrying a weapon I would have given little thought to forcing my interrogator into certain concessions. As it was, I pushed my hair back from my face and said, "No. He is not my lover. His wife is a friend of mine, she's staying with me."

"Yes. I met her yesterday. She was disturbed."

"Did you read the notebooks or not?"

"Do you have them?"

"No."

"But you are mentioned in them. That's the writing you were talking about."

"Yes."

He stood up. "I'll tell him you're here," he said. "If he wants to see you, he can. He may not want to." He paused at the door. "You see, I'm not unreasonable. But try not to upset him. He's excitable."

I nodded.

"Will it upset him to see you?" he asked.

I smiled. "It might."

"Are you sure you don't want to tell me what you want?"

"Positive."

He pointed to a mirror. "I'll have to watch you," he said.

"Go ahead."

He went out, closing the door behind him. I didn't think he was done with me, and expected him to come back and question me further. I was surprised when the door opened and Richard stood carefully poised in the frame. I felt suddenly shy, ashamed of myself for having come to this place, to be caught gripping the arms of a chair with both hands, feeling my stomach going weak. I couldn't look at him.

He closed the door and took a step toward me. "Helene," he said.

Was I about to collapse? My brain buzzed with the possibility, searching for an answer.

"I'm glad you came," he said. "But of course it's too late."

I phrased the question I had been worrying all morning. "How could you do it?" I said. "How could you give up your freedom?"

He shrugged his shoulders amiably. "Oh, that," he said. "That was nothing."

Our eyes met and I knew it was for the first time. Strength flooded into my legs, my back, down my arms to my fingertips. I hadn't expected this, to feel so happy to see him. His face was tired but his eyes burned as if they were lit from within. He smiled, a hopeless smile that could have meant anything, he was so riddled with insanity. It was in every line of his face, in the pathetic curve of his back and arms and in the tremulous hands he held out to me. I had never before noticed how small he was, how frail his bones were. I went to him, thinking only to look at him more closely. Our eyes didn't waver as I took his hands in my own, then moved easily through that gesture into another and another, until our bodies were pressed together and our arms were intertwined. I felt his hands moving down my back, pressing me closer to him, until I stood balanced on one leg, the other leg pulling upward, wrapping around his back. I clung to him and he to me. I thought we must pull each other down. From somewhere I could hear voices and the sound of footsteps. My own mouth was lost in Richard's, invaded by his tongue, which strangled me, strangled my thoughts. He had worked my blouse free from my skirt, and one hand slipped beneath it, over my ribs, closing tightly against one breast. My arms were around his back, tightening, pulling him down to me. We were falling, we would have to fall in this embrace to the floor.

Then I felt hands on my shoulder and other hands around my waist. There were voices, outraged, impatient, determined, and more hands pulling me away.

Richard was being pulled from the other side. We fought the hands and clung to each other, our mouths still pressed together. I didn't open my eyes until they had taken him completely from me. I saw him being pulled away, cursing them, trying to look over his shoulder at me, howling my name, until they had turned a corner and he was well out of sight. His doctor closed the door and gave me an incredulous look. I gave my attention to my clothes, which were badly disarrayed.

"I asked you to try not to upset him," he said.

"If you'd left us alone he wouldn't have been upset."

"I can't allow patients to screw in my office."

I picked up my purse. "No," I said. "I suppose not." I wanted to leave but he stood in front of the door. I had a premonition that it would be unwise to move toward him. I thought him far more dangerous than Richard. "I want to go now," I added weakly.

"Shall I tell his wife about this?"

"I don't care who you tell."

"Have you ever been in therapy?"

I laughed. "No."

He opened the door and stood beside it. "You should think about it. It might do you some good."

"I'm not so lost that I would ask a fool for directions," I said. My anger pleased and surprised me. I tried to appear resolute as I hurried out the door and down the stairs, but I knew I was moving much too fast and that he had seen how badly my hands were shaking.

When I got to the street I paid little attention to where I was going. I walked from the hospital to St. Charles, an eleven-block walk down a long tree-shaded sidewalk, past old, well-kept houses. I walked quickly, as if I were in a hurry. At St. Charles I caught a crowded streetcar. I had to stand in the aisle hanging on to a strap. I noticed knees, hands, faces around me and I thought the noise would deafen me. Gradually the car cleared out and I was able to sit down. I thought of Richard, back in his cell, probably receiving more sedation, and I knew that what made him mad was his willingness to give himself up to strangers. I blessed my own sanity, seeing for the first time what was at the core of it, my determination never to give up my freedom. I would never, never give up the option to walk away.

I felt a tightness in my chest and in my head, like strings pulled too tight, about to burst. You need rest, I told myself. You've been working too hard. You'd better rest, take a day off. Was I working too hard? Did I sleep enough? Eat enough? I tried to think of what I had been doing for the past week, yesterday, an hour ago, but nothing came clear for me. My eyes filled with tears I kept blinking back. I thought, Hang on now, calm down now, but behind this line of instruction I could hear myself reflecting that this was the way one spoke to a child, or to someone in whom one had no confidence. I began to make promises to myself. I wouldn't think until I got to Reed's. I allowed waves of anger and uncertainty to wash over me, mindlessly, like a woman in labor. Everything would have to wait until I got my body off the street.

After I got off the streetcar I had to walk twelve blocks through the Quarter. I chose Chartres because it was the most quiet, least threatening street. I counted my steps, starting over again every time I got to thirty or forty; I never knew just where because I kept losing count. In this way, keeping my eyes on the pavement before me, counting to keep from thinking, I arrived at Reed's apartment.

I was crying when he opened the door.

"Get inside," he said. I went in and he closed the door behind me. I was struggling against a terrific constriction in my chest.

"What is it?" he asked. I went into the bedroom and lay across the bed. "What's wrong, honey? What happened?"

"I can't talk," I said. I began to sob uncontrollably. I felt a knot in my throat tightening and breaking and tightening again. I got up and went to a chair.

"Try to tell me," he said.

"I've been at DePaul's," I said. "Richard's in there. He'll never get out."

"He cracked, huh?"

I covered my face with my hands. I was filled with revulsion. There was a whining sound in my throat, like an animal cornered.

"I haven't got much," Reed said. "I've got a few Seconal. Three ought to be enough." He went to a drawer and took out a container of red capsules, pouring them out into his hand.

"Take these," he said, coming to me. "It'll help."

"I don't want any," I sobbed. I got up and went to the corner of the room. I began to sway back and forth, tears running over my hands. I wanted to tear something, smash something. "Jesus," I said. "Oh, Christ."

"You don't have to shoot them," Reed said. "You can just take them with water." He held the capsules out to me.

New rage filled me. No wonder I'm frightened, I thought, I'm living in a world of suicides. I turned from the corner and slapped his hand so that the capsules flew out and scattered on the floor. I fell to my knees, moaning. When Reed bent over to help me up, I pushed him away. "Not me," I mumbled. "Not me."

"Well, if you won't take them, I will," he said. "I can't stand to watch this." He found two of the capsules immediately, then dropped to his hands and knees to search for the third.

"Good," I cried. "Go ahead. Maybe this time you'll kill yourself and be done with it."

"Here it is," he said. He swallowed the pills. "I know you're upset, but at least get off the floor and lie on the bed," he pleaded.

I tried to get up but couldn't. I fell back onto the floor. For a moment I lay there, pulling at my hair, mumbling incoherently. Then I turned on my side and drew my legs up, rocking back and forth to comfort myself.

Reed sat down beside me and pulled my shoulders into his lap. I didn't struggle. I sat up and he held me, rocking me back and forth. "Try to think of something else," he said.

I searched for a thought less painful. I saw Michael, laughing at something Clarissa was saying, turning to me contemptuously. Give that up, I thought and wept more bitterly.

"It's all right now," Reed was saying. "You're safe here."

"They're wrecking me," I said. "I can't. I'm lost."

"Did anybody do anything? Say anything to you?"

"I don't know what I'm doing," I said. "I make mistakes. I keep making the same mistakes."

"Honey, everybody does that. You do better than most. You're not suspicious. You're not mean." He paused. "You're the best woman I know."

"I'm weak," I said. "I'm spineless."

He pulled my back up so that he could hold me more tightly and pushed my hair out of my eyes.

"I know," he said, kissing my forehead and then my eyes. "Me too."

I began to calm down, to take comfort. It was a process I could feel. When my anxiety subsided I let it go, so that my feelings ebbed like a tide, each wave falling back behind the last. I thought of my desk in the office, of what was in the drawers, of the phone which was always, in my imagination, ringing insistently, and though I did not wish to go there, I knew I would. "I have to go to work," I said. "I don't have any leave left."

"In a little while."

"Do you think you could stop trying to kill yourself?"
I asked.

"I guess I could try."

"It's such an effort. Such a great effort."

"You want to start by getting off the floor?"

"Sure," I said. We got up and moved to the bed. I propped my back up with pillows and Reed rested his head in my lap. I stroked his hair until he drifted off to sleep. I knew I couldn't sleep and didn't attempt it.

It was quiet in his room and dark, the only sound the dull whining of the fan in the kitchen. My thoughts whirled and turned, colliding with one another and exploding like stars in a galaxy. I felt myself far from them, a distant, safe observer. I noticed that I had been sweating and that my skin was cool and damp. I pressed my thumb against my wrist and felt the pulse throbbing regularly. I considered the vast complexity of my own circulation and imagined the blood moving in me, streaming down my arms, bursting through the tiny veins in my fingers, rushing through my brain, pumping on and on, mysterious and soundless. The thought excited me and I was impatient, eager to move. I eased myself out from under Reed's weight and he turned away from me heavily, deep in sleep. When I sat up, the room spun about me, but I got to my feet anyway, clutching the edge of the mattress for support. By the time I reached the door, my vision had cleared and I hurried down the hall, anxious to leave the dark, dreamy gloom of Reed's apartment behind me and go out into the bright sunlight on the street.